Cat Tales for Mariette

Cat Tales

for

MARIETTE

An Unexpected Friendship
on the Camdeboo Plains
of South Africa

MICHAEL BROWN

namaste
PUBLISHING

Vancouver, Canada

Library and Archives Canada Cataloguing in Publication

Brown, Michael, 1962-, author
    Cat tales for Mariette / Michael Brown.

ISBN 978-1-897238-78-3 (paperback)

    I. Title.

PR9369.4.B758C38 2016   823'.92   C2016-901939-X 7

Published in Canada by
NAMASTE PUBLISHING
P.O. Box 62084
Vancouver, British Columbia V6J 1Z1
www.namastepublishing.com
contact@namastepublishing.com

Cover design by Diane McIntosh

Typesetting by Steve Amarillo / Urban Design

Printed and bound in Canada by Friesens

Dedication

For all the cats I've met, and especially
for my heart fish: Presence, Big Guy,
Chubbis Choppis, and Mrs. Botjie

As far as the cats are concerned,
everything written here happened.

Contents

Coffee Talk

In her late sixties, Cathy was just five feet tall, thin faced, but visibly muscular for her age. She had spent the first half of her adult life as a devoted nun, taking care of the convent gardens at Mariannhill Monastery.

That was until the day she inherited a huge estate— an event she decided was a sign from God to re-enter the world.

Cathy and I were introduced by a mutual acquaintance during my first year in Aberdeen, South Africa, and we instantly became close friends.

In our first meeting, she described how, after going on a mad spending spree, she had ended up in a mental institution. "A lot of money can make you very drunk," she chuckled. "I went from having two dresses to a walk-in wardrobe the size of the average person's living room. Eventually, I had to spring myself from that loony bin or be lost to the world forever."

At the time I met Cathy, she had property and business interests in various parts of South Africa, including a sugarcane farm in Natal and a winery in Stellenbosch. Nearing Christmastime, she took an annual road trip from one property to the other, always popping in for coffee with me along the way.

It was during one of these yearly visits that the subject of Christmas plans came up. "Are you doing anything this year?" she asked.

Anxious to brush the topic aside, I replied, "No, you know I don't do Christmas."

She smiled mischievously. "Is that because you don't like it?"

"Nope, I don't," I admitted. "And there are many poor people who don't like Christmas either. But only in January, when they've spent all their cash on unnecessary stuff that either gets broken in no time or exchanged."

Quietly puffing on her hand-rolled cigarette, Cathy looked at me intently. After several moments she said, "It sounds like you have some kind of unresolved emotional issue where Christmas is concerned."

She's poking at me because of the books I've written, I realized.

Then she challenged, "You should do something to change that."

Smiling at her ploy, I objected, "Why should I do something about it?"

She giggled. "If for no other reason, so you don't have to be glum once a year."

Defending myself, I countered, "I'm not in the least

bit glum. I find the whole thing somewhat annoying, that's all. But it definitely does not make me glum."

"Well, you're not exactly singing carols either, are you?" she retorted. Then, puffing on her smoke again, she recommended, "I think you should give yourself a special Christmas present this year, Michael."

"Oh, you do, do you?" I said, shifting on the bench on which I was sitting. "And what exactly do you have in mind?"

"Do something kind for someone you don't know," she suggested.

"Really? Oh, come on," I said, waiving the idea away. "Why on earth would I do that? That's just fiddling with people. It doesn't change them or solve their problems."

Despite my rebuttal, she insisted, "Do it so you can rediscover what Christmas is really all about."

"And what *is* it really all about, Mrs. Santa Claus?"

At that moment Presence appeared on the porch, jumping up onto the couch. "Hello *beautiful*," Cathy cooed as, after checking her out, Presence rolled on her side and up against my delighted visitor's leg.

As Cathy began stroking Presence's reddish beige fur, Presence closed her eyes, purring loudly. Rising from my seat, I announced, "I want to hear what you have to say about Christmas, but it's going to take a refill on the coffee."

I stepped into my cozy pale green kitchen, with its bamboo-covered ceiling and the customary Karoo house nook where a kitchen fireplace or wood stove used to be. This little room is heavenly to me. Through it comes all the nourishment that, despite my age heading the other way, enables me to feel younger as the days pass. Because of the abundance this room symbolizes in my life, it's a place where I often say aloud, "Thank you, God!"

This kitchen in which I stand and inhale the aroma of 100% Arabica is where all the work I'd done on myself to become less emotionally reactive and more fully present in my life had led me. Only God could have brought me on a journey that would arrive here, in this moment. Mine was the generation that ushered in the huge changes that came to South Africa, and many of my good friends are already gone, not having lived to see the first free and fair elections. Considering the state of this world, and how many of my friends are no longer here to enjoy 100% Arabica over intimate conversations, I feel deeply blessed.

"Oh, that smells good," Cathy exclaimed as I entered the living room and handed her a cup. "Delicious," she said, taking a sip. "You make the best coffee, Michael Brown."

"It's the one you brought," I informed her.

As I sat myself down again to enjoy my second cup of coffee with my guest, I felt the mid-morning sun warm my back. It was a particularly cool day for December in The Karoo. A magnificent semi-desert landscape blanketing the interior of South Africa, The

Karoo is a region of vast, rugged, beautiful emptiness that holds a mystique for city dwellers and tourists alike, Cathy being one of them.

Lighting a fresh smoke, she peered at me. "This thing you have about Christmas isn't really about Christmas itself," she announced. "It's actually about you."

She was right. During my first Christmas with my new stepfather, he had tried to win my brother and me over by buying us an overload of presents, and I hadn't responded to the gesture in the manner he had expected. Later that day, when he went out to check on a nearby farm, I gathered up the gifts and, going door to door with my bag like Santa, redistributed them among the little kids in a nearby Indian community.

You might be tempted to imagine I was being spiteful toward my stepfather by rejecting his gifts. Not so. I truly felt I had no need of all these toys and thought I was doing a good thing. Of course, when my stepfather arrived home, he was furious. To teach me a lesson, he made me go and retrieve each and every one of the gifts. To say the least, this was an awkward experience for a little boy. And just to reinforce the lesson, I got a spanking. From that time on, Christmas lost all appeal for me.

"Are you really proposing that I go around looking for someone I don't know to help?" I objected to Mariette's suggestion.

She smiled. "No, not exactly. But what you can do

is respond to Christmas rather than react to it." She winked.

Oh, I so dislike it when people use my own words against me!

"Instead of bemoaning the occasion," she continued, "ask that the Christ nature in you finds a way to be a useful presence to someone in need at this time."

I could see the nun in her still peeking through those lively eyes. In fact, the thought occurred to me, *It's obvious the nun part of you has never really retired.* Yet I have to admit that, the way she made it sound, the idea was almost inviting. It definitely stirred something within, maybe the child aspect of myself that hadn't been allowed to enjoy Christmas since the consequences of the overzealous young Santa Claus event.

Surprisingly, Cathy's next words took the form of a warning. "Be sincere Michael, or don't ask at all," she cautioned. "This is a Christmas prayer I'm asking you to send out. This is not a game. A prayer of this kind is *always* answered at Christmas, which means you can't be half-hearted about it."

Draining the last of her coffee, she explained, "I don't have to tell you that Christmas isn't about a particular day, sending cards, giving gifts, or even the tree. It's about experiencing the Christ presence and being a vehicle for this loving energy for someone in need."

By now I was a little uncomfortable. Attempting to shift the attention off myself, I asked, "Is this what *you* do each year?"

"Every year," she nodded, puffing away. "As Christmas approaches, I say, 'Christ, use me,' and every year something wonderful and unexpected happens."

"You get to do something for someone *every* year?"

"I do," she smiled. "And each year it leads to some sort of miracle—for them *and* for me."

Curious now, I inquired, "Have you already asked for this year's Christmas errand?"

She grinned. "I most certainly have. I ask at the end of November." Then, leaning forward, she said, "Look, I know for the most part that Christmas is driven by consumerism, but I choose not to succumb to all the hype."

"You sound like you're pretty serious about this Christmas stuff, Cathy."

"*I'm* not the one who's 'serious' about it. *You* are."

She was right again. I seriously didn't like Christmas.

"We live in a crazy world, but I refuse to let Christmas be what the world seeks to make it," she continued. "Christmas is here, Michael, and it's not going anywhere anytime soon. Since there's not much to be done about that, I make sure my Christmas experience is what *I* want to it to be."

Stubbing out her cigarette, she stood and stretched, announcing as she did so, "It's been good as always, my friend. However, I have a long drive ahead, so I best be off."

Having spent the night at a bed and breakfast in Uniondale or Middleburg, depending on which direction she was traveling, Cathy usually arrived mid-morning and stayed for about an hour. I looked forward to her visits.

Getting up too, I inquired, "So do you know what you have to do this Christmas? Has something happened yet to show you?"

Bag in one hand and keys in the other, she smiled. "Who knows? Perhaps that's why I had to stop and see *you*. Maybe you are my Christmas miracle this year."

"But you stop here on your way every year."

"Ah," she chuckled, "that's because you're a stubborn one, Michael Brown." She smiled. "Remember what I told you about *asking* to be useful? That part is up to you."

We embraced, said our goodbyes, and I stood and waved as she disappeared down Jackson Street, leaving a trail of dust behind her. I always felt a little sad to see her drive off, watching her ritually wave back to me one last time from her car window, then disappearing into a right turn.

I'm quite happy to be useful, I said out loud to myself as I locked the front gate, *as long as I don't have to travel anywhere.*

The Phone Call

I was glancing through my morning emails when the phone rang.

"Hello?" I said, picking up the receiver.

"Michael." It was Vicky, also known in the town as the BBC because of her capacity for gathering and broadcasting information. If you wanted to find something out, you just asked her. If she didn't know, she'd find out, report back to you, then also inform everyone in town.

"Sorry to bother you," she said, far too cheerful for that time of the morning, "but I heard some sad news and thought you might like to know."

It couldn't be all *that* sad, given her cheeriness. It's strange how having some bad news to pass on can cheer some people up.

"What is it Vicky?" I asked, not really wanting to know.

Her tone suddenly became grave with concern. "It's Mariette, Michael. You know, the lady you used to play bowls with, Mariette Van Wyk. She's in the hospital."

Still not really wanting to know, I nevertheless asked politely, "What's wrong?"

"Cancer." The dreaded word was followed by a deathly silence. I said nothing and waited for the inevitable full report. "She's had it on and off for a while, but apparently it's taken over and she's on her way out."

"I'm sorry to hear that, Vicky," I said. "Thanks for letting me know." Hopefully this would end the call.

It didn't.

"The thing is, I know you played bowls with her back when you used to play. Well, I was thinking, she really has no family or anyone. She's really all alone there in the hospital."

Vicky had arrived from Natal about a year after me. Like myself, she was considered an outlander by those born in Aberdeen. Only after ten years in this town are you considered a resident, and only after fifteen a local. Until then everyone watches you with dubious curiosity. Vicky's way of integrating herself into the town was to become the news bearer. Though she couldn't speak a word of Afrikaans, it didn't deter her from her self-chosen role. When her husband passed away, about two years after their big move, she made "Aberdeen" her full-time occupation.

Vicky had evidently been expecting me to say something about the predicament of someone dying alone in a hospital, but I had nothing to say.

"So I was just thinking," she barreled on after an

awkward silence, "what a nice thing it would be for you to go and see her. I know you don't know her all *that* well, and I realize you don't socialize much. But I think she would *deeply* appreciate a visit from you."

"Thanks again for letting me know, Vicky. I'll definitely think about it," I assured her.

I hadn't even replaced the receiver in its cradle before I knew I had been set up. It was early morning, and before the day could even start I had been ambushed by Cathy's idea of Christmas.

The First Visit

DECEMBER 11TH

There had already been a few instances in my life when I wanted to do something for a particular person but had left it too late. For instance, I once promised to send a relative a copy of Nigel Kennedy's *Four Seasons*. This relative has long since passed on and that CD is still on my shelf. It's there to haunt me a little, because sometimes I need that.

If Mariette Van Wyk was indeed dying, I would go see her. We had got along well back when I was attempting to integrate myself into the Aberdeen community by playing bowls. I had only fond memories of my encounters with Mariette and Pete, her late husband. They had made me feel welcome and included as I engaged with the more conservative Afrikaans elders of this town.

Mariette had been a superb bowls player. If you were the skipper and she was on your team, you always wanted her to play the number three spot in a four-person lineup. This was because she knew how to clean up any mistakes and simultaneously set up a good opportunity for the number four. She could always see the right shot to place, and she had a tendency to place it perfectly. Pete, her husband, had been a good number four. He knew how to place the winning shot. If you had them both on your team, you had it made.

During our moments together on the greens, which had always been filled with chatter and joking, I had come to know Mariette as a cheerful presence, if somewhat loud. Whereas she insisted on being instantly liked, Pete on the other hand was quiet and for the most part reserved. Except, that is, when they performed their Afrikaans folk songs with violin and banjo. Both were tone deaf, and neither had an aptitude for an instrument. If anything had endeared me toward this elderly couple, it had been the enthusiasm with which they performed so terribly. Those watching fought desperately not to laugh hysterically. I remember the first time they performed at The Aberdeen Bowls Club. It wasn't something you can forget. You're wounded for life after you witness such a spectacle—wounded in the most beautiful, beautiful way.

After a few months of fun, coupled with growing frustration with some of the town's conservative elders, I left the club. I had actually worked my way up the hierarchy to club secretary, as well as being a skip for the B team. Especially in a rural town as small as this, it's important to know where we fit in and where we really don't. I didn't feel at the time that I fit in at the bowls club and suspected my presence was more subtly disruptive than complementary.

Following this, just as people do in a small town, Mariette and I bumped into each other here and there. Whenever we did, we always stopped for a chat, and each time she asked when I was coming back to the bowls club.

Then, about a year ago, I heard she had lost her husband. It wasn't long after this that I learned she herself had become unwell.

I had seen her only once since then. She was in the line at the bank and appeared to be in good spirits. Other than this, I didn't know much about her, except that she was Afrikaans but spoke English well, and that she had worked behind the counter in the Aberdeen Post Office all her life but had retired quite a few years before I moved into town.

When I entered Mariette's private hospital room, she exclaimed with delight, her face a broad grin, "What are *you* doing here?" Reaching out her hand for mine, she smiled happily at my unexpected appearance, as we gently squeezed palms and held that position for a few moments.

The change in her appearance from when I last saw her was obvious. When I first met her a good few years back, she was a large, big-boned woman with long grey hair that she always tied up neatly in a bun. I imagine it rolled all the way down her back when she let it out. Although she was still big boned, she had much less flesh on her. As she grinned at me, I observed that she also still had all of her crooked teeth.

"Vicky phoned me and told me you were here," I began.

"*Dying*," she emphasized, laughing as she spoke. "I'm sure she's told everyone in town that I'm dying, because I suddenly had a lot of visitors, all of them looking sad and worried."

"I have every confidence she has," I assured her.

Then, without skipping a beat, Mariette asked, "You want tea?"

"Yes," I said, seating myself on the chair next to her bed. A cup of tea is always a good crutch to lean on when you don't really know what to say to someone.

I glanced around the room, which was clean, tidy, and quite empty. The sparse look reminded me of how much I hated hospitals. In addition to feeling awkward about visiting someone I didn't really socialize with, my general dislike for hospitals was one of the reasons I had hoped this would be a quick in-and-out visit. Inspecting the palms of my hands as if I had the ability to see germs, I thought about all the antibiotic-resistant infections people catch nowadays from what appear to be such sterile surroundings. I was in no mood for a superbug.

"Nurse," Mariette bellowed as one of the nursing staff passed in the corridor. "Bring us some tea, please. I have *another* visitor!"

Now that's the loud Mariette I remember, I told myself, breaking into a smile.

Rearranging her position, Mariette patted her palms down on the starched and ironed hospital bed sheet. Had I been in any doubt that she wasn't relishing the many hours she spent in this room, her next comment confirmed it. "If I didn't feel so hot today," she opined, "we could go sit in the garden and drink our tea there."

Small talk had never been my strong suit. Still, attempting to make conversation, I asked, "So have you really had a lot of visitors?"

"Quite a few. But they are all folks who will come only once, and then I'll never see them again."

My cheeks flushed as I experienced a rush of guilt. I definitely had no intention of returning either.

"So, are you....?" I asked hesitantly.

"Am I what?"

"Dying?"

"Yes," she declared without hesitation. "That's what the doctor says, and apparently it's happening quite fast." Though she was pale, she didn't look even vaguely deathly to me. "He said for me to get my affairs in order. I told him, 'Ja doctor, I wouldn't mind one quick affair before I go.'" She giggled at her own joke. "He also joked and said that such a thing would probably kill me. I said it would be a better way to die than this." Her face lost the amusement for a moment. "He's a very nice man," she added.

"It's cancer, then?"

"Ja, the *bloody* cancer. I first got the cancer in my stomach. They treated me, and it went away." Her tone turned momentarily dramatic. "Now the doctor says it's everywhere. I told him I won't do any more treatments, because I'd rather die naturally than be killed by the stuff they put in you." She laughed at her own joke again. "And, to be honest Michael, I would rather die at home, but the doctor says I need twenty-four-hour supervision. So here I am, in this bed, until the end." She patted her palms down on the white hospital sheet again, a noticeable nervousness leaking through her attempt to make light of the situation.

"How long did he say you have?"

"A few weeks," she replied matter-of-factly. "I asked him to be absolutely honest with me."

For a moment she was silent. Then, sounding serious again, she explained, "He told me it's going to get bad, then worse—and soon." Suddenly giggling, she added, "I asked him if he had any more encouraging words for me. I told him, 'I just want to see one more Christmas. That's all I ask.'"

She looked at me sweetly. "My husband, Pete, is gone one year already, you know. And we have no children. So I'm all right to go now. I'm ready." A smile creased her cheeks. "We had a very good life together."

I could see the emptiness left by Pete's departure echoing in her eyes. They had been one of those rare elderly, openly affectionate and inseparable couples, always holding hands like teenagers everywhere they went.

Glancing toward the door, Mariette sighed, "Ag, I hope I don't have to scream more than once for that tea. They did say I could order it anytime, day or night. I think they feel sorry for me, and giving me tea *anytime* is one way for them to deal with the fact I'm dying here in front of them and they can do nothing about it. There's no hospice in this hospital, either."

She smiled. "Besides, I would much rather be alone here in this small room than in the nursing home with all those old ladies and their blue hair." She patted her own head of hair, her long silver grey strands still beautifully rolled up in a bun.

"So, no more treatments for you, then," I said, trying to keep the conversation going.

"No, no more treatments. It's too hard. And anyway, I'm not losing my hair at this stage of the game. 'Just give me something for the pain,' I told the doctor, then let's get on with it."

Looking me in the eyes, she said with a smile, "You're probably surprised, heh? You probably expected to see a frail old blubbering scared wreck when you arrived here."

Vicky's phone call had certainly painted a picture of Mariette as lonely, isolated, and already halfway through death's door.

"Not really," I lied, grinning. "Remember, I've played bowls with you *and* against you, many times."

"That's true." Her eyes twinkled brightly at the memory. "Ag, I miss that. Bowls is not just for old people, you know."

"I know," I jested. "Look at me. I already retired from the game and I'm still a spring chicken." She smiled at my words, then suddenly appeared distracted. We sat in a comfortable silence until the sound of a tea trolley rattling along the corridor spurred her to move a few things around on her bed tray.

"Tea," she said softly. "I can't drink a lot of it these days, but I do enjoy the taste. I love the feel of the hot sweetness in my mouth." Then, lowering her voice to a whisper, she added with a wink, "But you have to make it right, and we can't expect *that* here in the hospital."

A nurse wheeled in the jangling trolley and placed two silver pots, one of tea and one of hot water, on the bed tray, together with a milk jug, two cups and saucers, teaspoons, a plastic bowl of white sugar, and a plate of cheap-looking cookies.

"Thank you," Mariette said, sounding most appreciative as the nurse left. Then, sitting back, she confided, "There will be things I yearn for once I leave this world, and I'm sure one of them will be tea. It's my food these days."

We sat quietly for some time, until the silence became uncomfortable. I didn't know what to say, and it appeared neither did she. After a while I asked, "Do you have any regrets?" No sooner were the words out of my mouth than I felt surprised by my question.

Mariette looked at me curiously. "Why do you ask?"

"I don't know, really. The word 'regret' just popped into my head, and so I thought I'd ask if you had any."

For an awkward moment she simply looked at me. Then she smiled broadly. "Thank you for asking, Michael." She adjusted herself in the bed. "Actually," she admitted, "I do have a regret—only one really, and it's silly."

"Why?"

"Because I miss something I never really had." She paused, visibly pondering the words she had just spoken. After a few moments she remarked, "How can you miss something you've never really had? Most people are trying to hold onto something they don't want to let go of, but for me it's different. For the past few days, I've been sitting here really saddened about something that *didn't* happen in my life. It's so small, but I can't deny the way I feel about it. I would have thought that if someone told me I only had a few weeks left to live, I might regret something I did or said to someone, but that's not what I regret. I regret something I *didn't* do—or rather, didn't have."

She looked at me, almost childlike, almost embarrassed.

"Oh come on, Mariette, you mean to tell me you're still a virgin?" I asked playfully.

Bursting into raucous laughter, she again slapped the bedcovers, this time not out of nervousness.

"No," she smiled, gathering herself. "That I am definitely not!"

"So, then tell me, what do you most regret?"

She hesitated, then took a deep breath. "I never had a cat," she said.

"What?" I gasped. "Really? That's what you would go back and change if you could?"

"Yes," she said earnestly. "I don't know why, but I feel that had I pursued my love of cats, which I've had ever since I saw my first kitten as a young child, my life would have been better. That's all—just somehow better."

"How so?"

"That's the thing," she said, her expression now saddening. "I can't say, because I never gave myself the chance to find out."

Leaning forward, she proceeded to pour the tea. "How do you take it?"

"Regular, I guess. Milk and two sugars."

She finished pouring and handed me a cup.

"Why do you think you never had a cat, given that you wanted one so much?" I asked, curious.

"I grew up on a farm where cats would just be dog food," she chuckled. "Then I married a man who promised me we could get some cats, but instead brought home two Maltese poodles. Naturally, I grew to love them, and they were with us for years.

After they died, he came home with a little crossbreed stoep-kakker, and that porch pooper also lived with us for years." She smiled, remembering. "That thing just made a noise and ran around in circles for no reason. But Pete loved the dog, so I put up with it. Soon after it died, Pete became ill. I decided not to have any more pets. I had enough on my hands taking care of him. I too hadn't been well, with the cancer."

She took a sip from her cup. "In my life, I have known a few people who owned only cats, and I was always so jealous of the stillness and peace in their homes. Being around a cat is always so very peaceful for me."

"Me too," I agreed.

"About a week before I was admitted here, when I started feeling a bit sick again, a beautiful black stray cat came to stay with me at the house. Well, he wasn't really a stray, because he was actually quite tame. I think he probably belonged to someone in our neighborhood, though I had never seen him before."

"Cats are known to sometimes have more than one home," I remarked.

"Really? I didn't realize that."

"When I was living in Tucson, Arizona, I was walking through my neighborhood one day when I spotted my cat, Cleo, sitting on the porch of a house four doors down. I called her and she came. As I was stroking her, a man appeared on the porch and said, 'She's a lovely cat, isn't she?' I told him she indeed was and that she had been with me for two years now, ever since I'd lived in San Francisco. 'You must be mistaken,' said the man. 'Millie Cat has been with us for about six months. She sits here on the porch with me every day.' I had noticed that Cleo was away a lot during the day. We both laughed when we realized that Cleo had decided she required two homes. That's what I like about cats—they *choose* to live with us. They can leave at any time, and some do."

"That's a sweet story, Michael," Mariette said with a warm smile. Then, giggling, she added, "I don't think you could tell a story like that about a stoep-kakker. Cats are more mysterious in some way."

"They're definitely otherworldly," I agreed.

She nodded. "I know what you mean. For the week I had that black cat around, I felt like my home had been transformed. For the first time in my life, I felt like I was living in an atmosphere suited to *me*."

She sipped her tea, thoughtful. Then she announced proudly, "So here I am, 79 years old, and only now I discover that I am, indeed, *a cat person.*" As she sighed, her eye's moistened. "And I guess the reason it's such a big regret for me is because I've been a cat person all my life, living among dog people, right until that last week in my home when that black cat came to stay." She smiled remembering. "With their peaceful yet playful presence, they really turn your home into heaven. But then my cancer came back, and I was brought here and told this is where I stay until it's over." She sat quietly for a moment. "You know, having that cat around me was like a last miracle from God for me, though it probably sounds silly to you."

"It doesn't sound silly at all," I assured her. "I'm a cat person too, and I can't imagine having lived my life without all the cats I've had in it. Were I to have cut out all the parts of my life that have had cats in them, I would have missed out on a lot of what have been the best parts of my life. They kept my heart open in some rough times."

"Really?" she said, evidently pleased by my words. "So you truly do understand what I mean?"

"I most certainly do," I assured her. "My cats are my immediate family. As I said, they kept my heart open when humans couldn't."

"I can believe that," she nodded. "I miss that black cat, even though I only knew him a short while."

"They sure know how to get straight into your heart," I confessed.

I had no idea what to say next, so we sat drinking our tea in silence. Glancing around for a clock, I realized there wasn't one. After a while Mariette asked, "Would you mind telling me another cat story?"

"Oh, I don't think I know any cat *stories*," I smiled, brushing away the idea.

"Well, I don't mean to put you on the spot, Michael," she said, "but you just told me a *very* good one. And you did say you were a cat person, so you must have some stories about the cats you've known?"

I smiled awkwardly.

"You know," she continued, "since leaving the farm, I haven't left this town. I remember when we first met you at the bowls club, how you told us about your travels. Surely you must have collected some stories along the way about the cats in your life?"

"Well," I said, my tone clearly resistant, "I don't think of them as *stories*." As pleasant a conversation as we had been having, I didn't want to sit in a hospital room any longer than I had to.

I sensed that Mariette could tell what I was feeling, and she looked disappointed. I felt bad. Reluctantly, taking a deep breath, I confessed, "I've had some interesting encounters with cats, that's for sure."

"Good." Her full smile returned. Pleading with the sweetness of a child, she said, "Then tell me another cat story, Michael. I have nothing to do but listen."

I surrendered. "Let's see," I said thoughtfully. "I honestly don't know where to start."

"Right at the beginning," she said excitedly. "Tell me about the first cat you ever met."

I had been ready to leave, and Mariette had picked up on this from my body language. Now, shifting in my chair, trying to appear as if I really wanted to be there, I said hesitantly, "Okay." Sitting back, I suggested, "What about a refill of that *delicious* hospital tea?"

Mariette's eyes smiled gratefully at my playful mock sarcasm, and she immediately reached out for my cup.

4

I'm a Cat Person

"From the time I was born," I began, "until I was about thirteen, I grew up in a dogs only world. I've been told I was born into a household with an Alsatian called Chaka, but I don't remember much about him. Apparently my brother and I slept on him—or was it him on us?"

Mariette smiled and handed me a fresh cup of tea.

"Chaka was apparently very protective of us," I continued, "and I suppose circumstances being what they were politically in South Africa at that time, that's what he was there for."

"For protection?"

"Yes, you could definitely say that. Anyway, a few years after my father died, my mother remarried a dedicated dog breeder. He came into our lives when I was about seven or eight, and from that moment on dogs were everywhere. His real love was the gun dog breeds. For him these were the Labrador, English Setter, Golden Retriever, and Cocker Spaniel. These were dogs with gentle, loving natures—well, except for the moody red-haired Cocker Spaniels. I loved them all, but strangely enough never did any one of them become *my* dog."

I paused to reflect for a moment. "I never really thought about that until now," I said, sipping my tea.

"That's because you're not a dog person," Mariette said enthusiastically, "but you just didn't know that yet."

"You're getting ahead of the story," I teased, pretending to be serious.

"Sorry," she chuckled, "carry on with your story. You said you never had your own dog."

"Actually, I don't recall ever wanting to have a dog of my own. There were always up to a dozen dogs around at a time, and often one of them was about to give birth to another litter of eight or so. I guess they were all *our* dogs, although I noticed how other members of my family became attached to particular ones. Anyway, my stepfather bred pedigree specimens for the show ring and for hunting, which they called field trials. His dream was to breed a dog that took first place as a show dog as well as a champion retriever. He always wanted to breed the most beautiful working dog ever, and for a short while he succeeded with a black Labrador Retriever champion called Rika. She was an amazing dog, beautiful *and* smart."

I peered into my teacup for a moment, remembering her.

"Go on," Mariette urged.

"Okay, so before I went to boarding school, I spent many a weekend at dog shows or field trial events, which I had no real love for or even an interest in. We pretty much had to be there to help with the dogs. My only consolation in going was that I might see a particular girl I had a crush on."

Smiling, Mariette winked.

"Other than that, I found no attraction in holding dogs on leads and picking up their poop."

Mariette shook her head, giggling. "There's the difference between dogs and cats right there," she declared. "Cats don't like to leave their business lying around for everyone to see. I saw how that black cat hid his away."

"Indeed," I agreed. "I figure that when it comes to cats and dogs, there are only four types of people in the world. There are cat people, dog people, people who like both cats *and* dogs, and people who like neither and may not even mind eating them."

"Euuw," Mariette said with a distasteful expression.

"I know," I agreed, chuckling. "I have found that cat people only like cats and merely *tolerate* dogs. Dog people on the other hand only like dogs and *don't* tolerate cats. Dog and cat people like dogs *and* cats, but then they also tend to like ducks and rabbits and guinea pigs too."

Mariette laughed heartily at my definitions.

"It takes all types," I said, "and there's definitely

peace in knowing what type we are, especially when it comes to dogs and cats. Cats are for the most part quiet, whereas dogs tend to bark just for the sake of it. Cat people generally don't like meaningless noise."

"That's true," Mariette agreed. "They tend to enjoy more solitude than dog people."

I couldn't resist what came out of my mouth next. "They don't like being taken out on leashes either. Which is why we cat people don't like to wear ties."

"You know," Mariette concluded, "for someone who claims to have no stories about cats and dogs, you have a lot to say about them."

I blushed. She was right. I sipped my tea, and Mariette sipped hers. Grinning and nodding at me to continue my story, she remarked, "So, you were saying you didn't like picking up the poop."

"Not just that. I didn't like the dog shows or the field trials or the hunting. As a boy, I enjoyed shooting guns for a while. But after I shot my first sparrow from my bedroom window, I never aimed at anything alive again, not even a tree. All in all, the doggy people my stepfather mingled with seemed a strange lot that I had no affinity with."

"So, where do the cats come in?"

"I'm getting to that right now. One afternoon when I was thirteen, my whole world changed. It happened as I explored the bushes beneath the lower grapevines of the vineyard we had moved to in Koelenhof, after leaving Natal. My stepfather was actually a chicken farmer, so we moved into a Dutch-style farmhouse close to one of the chicken farms he was overseeing."

"You were quite well off then?"

"No, we were a middle class farm management family. Since our home was on a farm, it was by far the best house we ever lived in. However, we rented it. There were vineyards as far as the eye could see, and there were also hills and overgrown areas as yet untouched by the winemaker's plough. It was in one of these untamed areas that I discovered a family of wild cats. The moment I caught sight of the protective mother and her playful kittens cradled in a nook by a dead tree and a forgotten irrigation ditch, I was entranced. For about two weeks, I returned eagerly every day after school. Gradually, the kittens became used to me. The mother remained ever wary, and I respected this. Although I desperately wanted to, I never touched any of them, even when they came close enough for me to do so."

"Ag, I'm sure they were *very* cute!"

"They definitely were. But this wasn't what attracted me to them. I felt different around them, as if something in me came alive. They seemed to remind me of something magical. Looking back, I would say they somehow opened my heart, and I really liked that feeling."

"That's exactly how I felt when that black cat was around me," Mariette agreed. "Whenever I was with him, I felt softer inside. So, what happened next?"

"One afternoon, I couldn't see the mother cat anywhere. The kittens were playing happily, chasing each other in and out of their safe hidey hole. I had visited them once or twice before when their mother had been away. I figured she was probably out hunting, so I thought nothing of it. However, the next afternoon, the kittens weren't playing. Looking cautious and distressed, they seemed skittish and stayed closer to cover, meowing for their mother. The following afternoon, they came running the moment I approached, meowing repeatedly. For the first time, they let me pick them up."

"The mother was missing."

"Yes. It was obvious they hadn't been cleaned and were hungry. When I ran home and reported the situation to my mother, she said to get a cardboard box and bring them to the house. She also warned me to be careful the dogs didn't get them. I remember Jackson, our gardener, had to confine certain of the dogs in their kennels because they wanted to get into the box when I arrived."

"What did you do with the kittens?"

"I took them into the bedroom I shared with my brother and made a safe space for them in an open cupboard. Then I gave them some water and puppy food. My mother was firm about what had to happen, though. 'We have to find a home for them immediately or take them to the SPCA,' she declared."

"They couldn't stay with you?"

"I asked the same question, pleadingly, but all

the time knowing full well they couldn't. My mother insisted, 'Absolutely not, the dogs will kill them! We can't have cats in *this* house—you know that.' We kept the kittens for a few days before they were taken to what I was assured was 'a very good home.' I think they really went to the SPCA."

"Were you sad when they left?"

"I'm sure I was," I said, trying to recall. "What I do remember is thinking how strange it was that while they were there in our bedroom, everyone came to look at them just once and said they were cute. But no one really wanted to go near them or help me take care of them. While they were there and I was home, I seldom left the room, and my family seldom entered. From the look in their eyes when the kittens first arrived, they might as well have been fluffy rats or even spiders or rabbits."

I smiled, remembering. "I also recall everyone's quiet relief when they were gone, like something slightly untoward had at last been dealt with. From the day the kittens left my room, so did something I felt strangely akin to—something that was somehow more like me than dogs were. Despite being brought up in a dog world, this brief encounter with cats was a revelation for me. I was *not* a dog person, although I hadn't known this until I met that family of cats."

"You see, I told you," Mariette enthused. "You're lucky—you discovered you were a cat person early on."

"You're right," I agreed. "If I think about that encounter now, it was actually life-changing for me, though in a subtle way."

Mariette smiled, pleased. "Tell me how."

"From that moment on, I gravitated to any cat that crossed my path. If I entered someone's home and a cat presented itself or was watching close by, it was always greeted and even approached. That beautiful wild mother and her kittens definitely reflected back to me an aspect of myself I hadn't known existed. Before they came into my life, my world was devoid of a mirror for this part of me."

I fell silent for a moment, then remarked, "That's quite interesting, I think."

"What?"

"That you can't know something about yourself until you see a reflection of it in the world around you to remind you of it. It was the real, in-the-moment, intimate encounter with these creatures that I was attracted to. You know, the heart-opening feeling they create."

Mariette smiled and nodded.

"Cats are very intimate," I continued, "and I don't think my love for cats is simply a matter of my wanting something I wasn't allowed to have as a child. I considered that possibility, but I don't believe it was the case."

I grinned. "I was born a Leo," I said, "for whatever that counts for. Anyway, from the time I left my parents' home, I never stayed where there were dogs if I could avoid it. It's not that I don't like dogs. I get along with them. But from the time I was able to have my own private space, I've only had cats around me."

"I think you're right," Mariette said reflectively. "That mother and her kittens did show you something about yourself."

"They definitely showed me we're not all the same," I said, "and that our hearts connect with different things. My stepfather loved dogs, possibly more than humans, and my love for cats has taught me it's all the same love."

"Did you feel different from your family when you were growing up?"

"Yes, I did. But I'm starting to think most people do."

"You might be right about that."

"In fact, for a long time I suspected my brother and I had been adopted. Then I thought, 'No, it's just *me* who was adopted.' But none of this was true. What was true is that I felt different from my family in a way I couldn't explain. It wasn't due to adoption—it was because they were all dog people!"

We laughed together.

"There's a saying that sums it up," I added. "The difference between cats and dogs is that cats have staff, whereas dogs have owners."

Though Mariette smiled, I could see she was becoming tired.

"That's because dogs have to be fed, whereas cats just like being served," I said.

"That's good," she replied softly. "I like that." She was quiet for a moment, then reached out her hand. I stood to take it.

"This was fun," I said.

"I would carry on talking with you, but I suddenly feel a bit tired," she said, her eyes heavy. "I wonder, would you be able to come tomorrow in the early morning, before it gets too hot? We can sit in the garden and you can tell me how this story ends."

"It's not really a story. But okay, tomorrow morning then." It just wasn't in my heart to deny her.

"Oh," she said, looking down at the plate in front of her, "I forgot to offer you a cookie."

5

Black Cat Days

DECEMBER 12TH

It was the first time I had seen the back of the hospital from the grounds themselves, though I'd seen it often enough from the adjoining Aberdeen Golf Course as my mother and I walked her dogs, Magnum and Minky. The garden we were to meet in that morning was simple but well taken care of. Aside from the concreted area by the washing line with its sheets flapping, it consisted of mowed lawn and a few garden beds, with just one large mesquite tree for shade. The area was hedged in with spekboom, the Afrikaans name for elephant bush, an evergreen shrub or small tree.

I found Mariette sitting in the dappled sunlight of the mesquite's shade, its tiny fluffy yellow flowers dripping with bees as they buzzed against the dark green background of petite feather-like leaves. Curled up comfortably to one side in her wicker lounge chair, she appeared to be asleep.

Since I still felt a resistance to being there, I decided not to wake her and sat down. *If she keeps on sleeping,* I told myself, *I'll quietly slip away.* Thankfully the garden offered a magnificent view of The Camdeboo Mountains, an ancient and majestic feature in our part of The Karoo.

I was thinking of the bittersweet taste of the tiny plump spekboom leaves, when Mariette shifted in her chair. "Would you be a honey and pour your own tea today, Michael," she said dryly, without opening her eyes. "I feel a bit tired, but I'm so glad you came. I have been thinking about your story."

I saw that the hospital staff had already brought tea. I poured myself a cup and sat down. "Actually, since our visit yesterday, I've been thinking about my life with cats," I said. "Not just cats that have lived with me, but cats that have come around at times. I didn't realize what an important part they have played in my life until I actually stopped to ponder it."

Mariette remained still and quiet, so I suggested, "If you're tired, maybe I should come another time."

"Oh no, you're not escaping *that* easily," she said, opening her eyes and winking at me. I noticed how exhausted she looked—and, more than the day before, how frail she really was.

"I'm sorry," I said, "I didn't even ask how you are doing."

"I'm *dying*," she said, smiling, "and so you don't ever have to ask how I'm doing, *okay*?"

"Okay." I understood completely. Everyone who came to visit her probably asked that. Her tone made it quite clear I wasn't there to talk about her health.

"It's strange how life is, Michael," she continued. "One moment I was standing on the bowls green with Pete, enjoying myself, and the next I'm here, Pete is gone, and the game is over. Sometimes it's a lot to take in. Usually when life takes a difficult turn, you can do something to take your mind off it, like gardening or going for a walk. Now, there's nothing to distract me from what's happening to me. And although I sometimes feel him around me, Pete isn't here anymore to hold my hand."

There was nothing to add to the truth of her words but silence, so that they could be truly heard and felt.

"So," she said after several moments, "tell me what important things happened in your life around cats."

"Two things come to mind. Both happened around the same time, which makes them interesting. And both involved black cats."

She winked again. "Like the one that came to stay with me."

"Yes," I said, smiling at her playfulness.

"Go on," she encouraged.

"I've heard people say it's unlucky when a black cat crosses your path. But what if you are already having a *really* bad day when that happens?"

Intrigued, Mariette nodded for me to continue. "Tell me."

"This happened in June 1980, at the end of my first six months at the University of Cape Town. I didn't enjoy my classes, and on that particular day, I was convinced I was having the worst day of my life. I had finished attending the day's lectures, which had either befuddled or bored me. Arriving back at my bicycle, I discovered I had a puncture. Since I had no bicycle pump and only a few cents in my pocket, I realized I would have to push the damn thing all the way back to my accommodation. The people I was staying with were doggy friends of my stepfather. They were big into dog shows, proudly parading their animals and looking important. But when they were home, it was a different story. They let mold grow on the edge of their dog's drinking bowls, they were loud and always far too jovial, and the woman bordered on maniacal at times. I loathed being there. I hated even more the idea of having to walk the three kilometers back with a punctured bicycle tire."

Mariette nodded understandingly.

"When I was about halfway there, I noticed a pitch black cat rolling in the sunshine on a grassy island between the left and right lanes. It was so beautiful, it looked like a miniature panther. Happy to be distracted, I propped my bike against an old oak and strolled over to say hello. We hit it off immediately, which resulted in a fest of stroking and purring. Then, without warning, the sleek grass-covered creature darted off across the road and into a coffee shop.

Counting my change, I realized I probably had enough for a cup of coffee, so I followed the cat inside."

"This sounds mysterious," Mariette said, looking pleased.

"Just wait, it gets better," I said, setting my teacup down on the metal side table next to me. "I no sooner sat down with my coffee and began rolling a cigarette than a taxi drove up and stopped in front of the place. I noticed that the passenger was sitting in the front seat next to the driver, which seemed a little odd. Anyway, the driver came in and asked the man behind the counter whether they served vegetarian food. The man responded that they could make any sort of salad sandwich. The driver went back out and leaned into the passenger window, whereupon the passenger disembarked and joined him in the cafe. Though he was sitting with his back to me, he was angled to the side so I could see his profile. His hair was tied back in a ponytail, kind of cool, and somehow he looked familiar."

"Who was he?"

"That's the problem. I recognized his face, but I also had no idea who he was. Then he turned around and caught me staring at him. I obviously couldn't turn away, and he broke into a huge grin. All I could do was smile back—and for what felt like a long time, we just sat there smiling at each other, without either of us seeming to feel the need to say anything, not even hello."

"So who was it?" Mariette said, sounding insistent.

"Wait, I have to get there."

Mariette giggled, delighted.

"This is the strange part that has never made sense to me. The next thing I remember is looking at the burned-out cigarette between my fingers, which I'd hardly puffed on, then at the untouched cup of coffee on the table in front of me. The table where the two men had sat was empty—they had apparently already eaten and left. I felt disorientated and even a little scared. Had I perhaps blacked out? But as I looked around, the man behind the counter was busy with a customer as if nothing had happened, and the two other people at another table nearby were still chatting away. For a moment, I wondered whether I had imagined it all, though I knew I hadn't."

"What did you do?" Mariette pressed.

"I took a sip of my coffee and discovered it was lukewarm. Obviously it had been sitting there a while. This disturbed me even more. Relighting my smoke, I sat gathering my thoughts, then eventually got up and went outside. The first thing I noticed was the black cat back on the grassy island, rolling on its back, paws outstretched back and front, still covered in bits of grass and enjoying the last of the afternoon sun."

I smiled and sat back. "Now this is where it gets good."

Mariette leaned forward ever so slightly.

"The following evening, my annoying landlady came banging loudly and excitedly on my door. I remember I was sitting on my bed feeling sorry for myself. 'Come in,' I said, not for a moment letting the tone of my voice hide the fact I wasn't at all interested in seeing her. 'You won't believe it, Michael,' she burst out, waving The Cape Times newspaper. 'Look here on the front page! John Lennon was in Cape Town yesterday. He spent the entire day with a taxi driver who took him to see all the sites, even up Table Mountain. Fancy that—nobody even knew he was here."

"Wow," Mariette exclaimed. "You met John Lennon and didn't even know it!"

"How about that," I said, a big grin creasing my cheeks. "A most magical thing happens to me on a day when I think my life completely sucks, but I don't find out until afterward."

"How did it make you feel when you found out?"

"Actually, I think I cried. In fact, now that I recall, I'm sure I did."

"Why?" she asked, a little surprised.

"I think I felt that for this to have happened to me, well, it somehow meant I couldn't be a complete nobody-loser. It made me feel like something was trying to show me that somebody knew I was alive. Because it was a time when I wasn't feeling seen by anyone, I guess it made me feel special."

"What do you mean?"

"When I saw that punctured tire on my bike, I felt deflated. Yet if that hadn't happened, I wouldn't have got a smile from John Lennon."

"And it was the black cat crossing your path that led you in there!" Mariette noted.

"It was," I nodded. "Which is why I gleaned an important lesson from that strange non-encounter."

Mariette appeared curious, cocking her head to the side with a wry smile. "What did it teach you?"

"That no matter how bad a day I may be having, if a black cat shows up, I need to pay attention. I also now keep in the back of my mind that I may already be in the middle of something fantastic and just not know it yet."

"That's a good feeling to have anytime," Mariette affirmed. Then, carefully standing, evidently weak, she requested, "Would you mind moving my chair further into the shade? I like the warmth, but I can't take the direct sunlight, even this early, and it's going to hit me any moment."

Getting up, I moved her chair deeper into the partial shade of the mesquite.

Sitting down again, she urged, "Have more tea."

I obediently helped myself. As I reached for the teapot, she inquired with a tone of mild amusement, "What was the other thing you said you thought of that involved a black cat?"

I finished pouring, pulled my chair closer to hers, and sat down. "This next thing happened about a week later, just a week or two before our university term ended. I was with about a hundred other students in a large lecture auditorium waiting for the professor to arrive. I knew only a couple of the students in that class, and this was only because I was in high school with them. Up to this point in my life, I had been largely invisible. The truth is, I was socially introverted, and consequently usually had only one trusted friend at a time."

"You haven't changed much," Mariette teased.

"I guess I haven't," I said. "But back then I was more extreme. I remember being uncomfortable in most social settings. Unless I had to, I definitely didn't socialize with groups, and I didn't play sports unless it was compulsory. This was why I'd been at UCT six months already and still not really met anyone. I kept to myself, coming and going without hanging around on campus any longer than I had to. I hadn't yet moved into the student hostel, which was something that wasn't going to happen until the beginning of the next term."

I took a sip of tea before continuing, "The professor was quite late that day, but he eventually entered quietly from the side door and mounted the steps onto the large stage. The teaching venue appeared to double as a theater, since it also had stadium seating. As the professor shuffled through his worn brown leather briefcase for papers and books, a black cat strolled casually out onto the stage from my right and seated itself next to him."

"And was it also a beautiful black cat?"

"It was indeed," I confirmed. "Of course, as this

cat came out and sat there next to the professor, every-one chuckled. Then, when they realized that only the professor was unaware of the cat, and that he had no idea why we were giggling, they broke into laughter. He no doubt thought we were laughing at him because he was late, but soon he realized we were laughing at something he couldn't see. Finally, looking down to his left, he noticed the cat sitting there quietly, right next to him. Leaning into the microphone, he quipped, 'If I had been any later, he probably would have started the class without me.' We all had a good laugh. The subject of the class was Management of Human Resources, and the cat, without doing any-thing, seemed to be doing a very good job of this."

"What happened next?"

"We were all captivated as the cat sat patiently, as if waiting for the professor to get his teaching materials together. Then, just as the morning lecture commenced, it stood up and walked to the center of the stage, right in front of the professor, where it paused for a few moments surveying the watching faces before finally lying down like a Sphinx overseeing its empire. This time the professor joined in the laugher and raised his hands in surrender. 'How can I compete with such a performance?' he declared. So the cat remained statu-esque in this position, the laugher died down, and the lecture began. Yet all eyes remained on the cat."

"I can imagine the scene," Mariette said, "like you *can't* look away."

"Yes," I said, nodding. "It was exactly like that. I attempted to listen to the professor, but of course ended up watching the cat."

"Did it stay for the entire class?"

"Yes, but it didn't confine itself to the stage. A little way into the lecture, it got up, vaulted gracefully off the stage, and strolled up the isle—of course, with all eyes monitoring its progress. Eventually the professor stopped talking and watched with us, equally enchanted. Our eyes followed the cat all the way up the stairs, until it came to the row in which I was sitting. It then turned into the row and began gliding in my direction, weaving in and around the feet of those in its path. Everyone, including me, wanted to know where the cat was so intent on heading. The next thing I knew, it was right at my feet."

Mariette's gaze was fixed on me. "What did it do?"

"It looked up at me, jumped onto my lap, circled around once or twice to ascertain the best position, then curled up, closed its eyes, and drifted off to sleep, purring loudly."

"And what did you do?"

"When I looked up, I realized everyone was now looking at me with considerable curiosity. 'And who might you be, oh great cat man?' the professor asked playfully over the PA system. 'Michael Brown,' I replied hesitantly."

"Wow," Mariette said excitedly. "Did the cat stay on your lap long?"

"It stayed for a good part of the lecture, then quietly hopped down and left. But from that moment onward, my experience on campus changed drastically."

"What do you mean?"

"When I went to venues such as the university cafeteria, people who were vaguely familiar, along with complete strangers, came and sat at my table, starting conversations with me. Naturally, this was something new to me. From that day on, people in the class greeted me by my full name. One day I was a nobody who knew no one, and the next people were greeting me with, 'Hello, Michael Brown.' They behaved as if they knew me, and strangely I didn't mind it. After all, the only thing that had really happened was that a black cat had curled up on my lap and fallen asleep."

"Ag, Michael, I love these stories of yours. Thank you for sharing them," Mariette said, smiling sweetly.

"I didn't really know I had such stories," I confessed. "There are likely more. As I said earlier, it wasn't until telling you about them that I realized what an important part of my life cats are."

Mariette looked pleased as she confided, "Your cat stories are like a painkiller for my mind."

In my mind's eye, I saw myself locking the garden gate after Cathy's departure. *I'm quite willing to be useful, as long as I don't have to travel anywhere*, I had said out loud as I walked back to my porch. As the Aberdeen hospital was a twenty-minute walk or few minutes drive from my front gate, it was now obvious to me that I was sitting inside an unfolding Christmas miracle.

Since there was nothing compelling waiting for me back home, and Mariette so evidently appreciated the distraction from her pain, I continued, "Now that I think about it, I received another surprise following this experience. Despite having terrible grades in every class during my year-and-a-half stint at UCT, I received the highest grade awarded in that particular class. I remember that it was 97%. I remember because I had never achieved 97% in anything."

"That's very good," Mariette congratulated me.

"Thank you," I smiled. "I thought so too. The funny thing is, I don't remember liking the subject that much. But maybe it wasn't about that. Maybe it was about how I felt while in this particular lecture theater after that cat baptized me with its attention. Also, now that I think about it, the cat encounter affected my socializing."

"In what way?"

"After the holidays, I moved into Leo Marquard Hall, the university student residence. A couple of evenings into my stay, there was a knock on my dormitory door. Hovering in the hallway was someone I vaguely knew from the same class in which the black cat had singled me out. 'Coming to join us for supper, Michael Brown?' he asked cheerfully. 'No thanks,' I answered in my old introverted way. 'I have some stuff to do before I go down,' I lied. 'Okay,' he said, smiling, and went on his way. I remember standing there for a moment, frozen in my own predictable past behavior. Then, out of the blue, I took a deep breath, stepped to the doorway, and shouted down the passageway after him, 'Hang on, I'm coming!' I remember the moment so vividly because I was consciously choosing another way of being."

"That was quite a switch for you, Michael."

"Indeed it was. Instead of opting to be alone, I willingly joined a table of eight people who all became good friends for the duration of my stay at the university. Through them, I met so many other wonderful people, some of whom I'm still in contact with today."

Mariette smiled. "It must have been the change in the way you engaged with people on campus after the black cat encounter that gave you the confidence to break your pattern of social isolation. When did that pattern start?"

"I have always been somewhat introverted, but it intensified during my high school boarding school experience," I related, looking down at my teacup and saucer as I spoke. "There's no doubt in my mind that had that black cat not curled up on my lap at such a timely moment, I would have declined the invitation of new friendship, or maybe not even have been invited. Then I would have missed out on so much."

I looked up and was surprised to see Mariette's eyes filling with tears. "It's okay," she assured me. "It's just that your story brought to mind that maybe I didn't make such brave choices in my life." She sniffed. "Many times I went one way, when I could have gone another. It's the thought of what I may have missed out on that makes me feel so sad."

"I know what you mean," I said comfortingly, "but we can never know."

"You are very blessed, Michael Brown. You know that, right?"

"I do," I agreed. It was something she would remind me of more than once as our visits continued.

Mariette blew her nose loudly enough to startle a group of nearby pigeons, which instantly took to the air.

"Good," she continued. "And I appreciate your coming here and sharing your stories with me. Can you come again tomorrow?"

"Yes," I said, glad to feel I meant it this time. There was something about telling these cat stories to Mariette that was also comforting to me.

She reached out, and I got up to place my hand in hers. "Be a good man and tell any nurse you see to come help me back to my room."

"I can help you," I offered.

"No, you aren't here to do that. You're here to tell me about your life with cats, okay?"

"Okay."

I left her beneath the branches of the shady mesquite and made my way home along the dusty roads of Aberdeen. I knew Mrs. Botjie would be waiting near the gate for me, and she was. I felt a renewed appreciation for her and all the cats that had come into my life over the years.

6

Spirit Watching

DECEMBER 13TH

It was a beautiful Karoo summer morning, not yet scorching, though already warm enough to appreciate shade. My mother was currently away visiting my sister Fiona and her husband Alan at their beach cottage in Chintsa, just outside East London. So before going to see Mariette, I popped into my mother's house to check on her pot plants.

While I was there, I also watered her vegetable garden, then stopped for a chat with Magnum, who's now buried there. Magnum and I were friends. He was a male dog, and I was the only male consistently around him, so he bonded with me. He drove me crazy as much as he melted my heart. Just as I never imagined I would end up living in a town like Aberdeen, I never imagined I would come to love a Doberman Pincher.

It occurred to me that it had been some time since I had last walked the golf course, so I elected to stroll up to the hospital on the fairways. It's the only golf course I've seen whose fairways are Fynbos and gravel, and whose greens are comprised of compressed sand mixed with tar. There's often no green to be seen on the entire course.

I arrived early, only to find Mariette not in the garden but propped up with pillows in her bed. "It feels too hot to go outside today. I hope you don't mind," she apologized as I entered the room.

"That's okay," I said. "Besides, I brought us some of Madeleine's carrot cake from Vroutjie Se Koutjie. It's spiked with banana and coconut."

"I'll have a taste," she said, looking gingerly at the cling-wrapped slice. "I can't even eat these bloody cookies anymore." Then, forcing a smile, she chided herself, "But no moaning from me while you are here, I promise." She reached out and we squeezed hands. It was clear she was feeling poorly.

"You can moan as much as you like," I joked. "I'll just ignore you."

Her expression warmed, she winked, and I sat down.

Pouring the tea, Mariette shifted the conversation to what she really wanted to hear, remarking, "There's something mysterious about cats and something magical about your stories. When a cat enters a room, like in your story, they have a studied manner to them. They glide in. Then they usually make for someone in particular, just like in your last story."

"You're right," I agreed. "They are indeed calculating in everything they do."

Mariette finished preparing the tea and carefully cut me a piece of the cake. "You're like that too, Michael Brown. Each time you visit me, you glide in here *very* quietly, appraising everything that's going on before you settle in."

I smiled.

"I also know that you aren't interested in anyone else here, just me," she said with a wink.

"That's true," I admitted, noting she hadn't poured any tea for herself. Neither had she gone any nearer to the carrot cake than had been necessary to cut a slice for me.

"Tell me about the first cats you had after you left home," she requested as I picked up my teacup, "the very first ones that came to live with you."

"Hmm, let's see," I said, thinking back as I took a sip of tea. "The first two kittens I brought home with me were called Willow and Maya. I chose them from a litter of seven. They were black sisters with white paws, each with a white splash on the face and white-tipped tails. They were gorgeous."

"What breed would they be?"

"You know, I've never thought about cats in terms of their different breeds, just like I have no interest in Latin plant names." I grinned, adding, "I guess they were regular thoroughbred black and white house cats."

"Did you love them immediately?"

"I did. From the time they came to live with me, coming home became a quite different experience— life-changing, in fact, as I mentioned the other day. For me, cats make a house a home. These cats came to live with me when I was staying in an apartment near Yeoville. I was against getting any cats as long as I lived in this Johannesburg suburb because I had no garden. However, I had just upped my income, since I was now working as an assistant editor for a music magazine. I figured I would eventually move into a house with a garden, which I did quite soon after. I had a friend in the A&R department of a record company who was a cat lover. When I expressed an interest in having a cat, she said, quite sternly, 'A cat alone just doesn't sit right with me.' She insisted I get two so they would have each other for company when I was away, and it sounded like a good idea. She was also the one who told me of the litter from which Willow and Maya came. Willow was more self-contained and reserved, whereas Maya was somewhat more outgoing, though also a little needy. They loved each other, and they loved me."

I fell silent for a moment as a memory flooded back to me. "Now that I think about it," I continued, "I had a strange experience with them shortly after they arrived."

Perking up, Mariette inquired, "What happened?"

I took a bite of cake and felt an expression of delight appear on my face. "Well," I said, chewing and swallowing, "I think it was just a few nights after I got them. I was awoken from sleep and found myself startled, as if someone had tapped me on the shoulder. Raising myself on my elbows, I glanced around the room. I saw the two kittens silhouetted in the streetlight streaming through my window and across my bed. Evidently I had fallen asleep without closing the blinds. Willow and Maya were on each side of my feet, at the end of the bed, both sitting on their haunches—like *really* sitting, their heads moving in sync, seemingly watching the same thing in the room. But I could see nothing."

When I paused to take another sip of tea, Mariette implored, "Don't stop there! Tell me what happened."

"Naturally, I observed them with fascination—and at the same time somewhat with disquiet. I watched their eyes follow something I couldn't see. Whatever it was, it had the full attention of both Willow and Maya. I watched their heads turn in sync as 'it' moved past the end of my bed. I observed how totally alert they were as they traced its movement all the way to my front door. I actually felt the hairs on the back of my neck stand up. Then, at the same instant, both cats sat back down. They continued to watch the door for a little while, then finally curled up and went back to sleep. I have to admit, *I* didn't go back to sleep so easily."

"Wow!" Mariette chuckled, her face alight with excitement. "That's almost a ghost story! You had me going there for a moment. I'm not good with scary stuff."

Then, looking across at the teapot, she said, "I

think I might just have some of that tea now." Pulling herself into an upright position, she reached for the teapot and began to pour.

She was about to take a sip of her tea when I remarked, "It doesn't end there."

"No?" she blurted out, setting her teacup down without drinking, clearly riveted by the story.

"Next morning at the office of the magazine I worked for, I received a phone call telling me that a close and dear friend, Raymond Erickson, had passed on the previous evening from an asthma attack."

"Oh, my goodness!" Mariette exclaimed, raising both hands to her mouth in shock. "It *is* a ghost story."

"Just not a scary one," I said, my eyes moistening at the thought of my friend's passing. "Apparently he stopped by to say goodbye."

"Just think," Mariette said, "if you hadn't had the kittens, you might never have known. Now I *am* going to have some tea." She picked up her teacup and took a sip. Then, speaking as if she was talking to herself, she announced, "That's proof right there."

"Proof of what?"

"That I'm not ending," she said decisively, her eyes moistening. We sat in silence for a while, which afforded me an opportunity to savor the rest of the carrot cake.

7

Portaling & Telepathy

"**D**id you have any other strange experiences with Willow and Maya?" Mariette asked, breaking the silence that had descended on the two of us.

For a moment I was thoughtful, remembering back. "I suppose that depends on what you mean by 'strange.' The first time I became aware of a cat's ability to move through portals would qualify, I guess. That was definitely with Willow and Maya."

"What do you mean by *portals*?"

"The only way I can explain it is that cats can seem to move in and out of invisible doorways."

"Are you saying you saw Willow and Maya become invisible?"

"No," I laughed, "just the opposite. It's like they would be invisible, and then suddenly reappear. When I had Willow and Maya, I never lived in large places, so it wasn't hard for me to look everywhere for them when I happened to notice they weren't around and wondered where they were. I looked only because they *felt* gone. I learned that whenever I had this feeling, either one or both of them *were* gone. Though I searched everywhere, they were usually nowhere to be found, and I would finally give up. Almost instantly, I would see whichever of them was missing sitting casually by my feet as if they had been there all along."

"Was this something that happened often?" Mariette asked quizzically.

"It happened too often for it to be coincidence. When I first began noticing it, I mentioned it to my cat-loving friend in the A&R department. She was amazingly casual about it as she explained, 'They do that all the time, Michael. They know passageways from far away that open up right by your feet. To this day, all my cats do this.' When I asked her how long they were gone, she said nonchalantly, 'I don't know. I just know they get back instantly. Not quickly, *instantly.* One moment they're not there, and the next they are.'"

Mariette's jaw had dropped.

"Come to think of it," I continued, "once Willow was gone for about three weeks. Naturally, I was distraught. I searched for days. After two weeks, she felt so gone that I let go of all hope of ever seeing her again. In fact, I mourned her. Then one afternoon while I was frantically typing away, chasing a deadline for the music magazine I worked for, she quite casually walked through the room as if she'd never been gone, heading for her water bowl. At first I assumed it was

Maya, until Maya appeared, equally casually, to sniff her butt."

Mariette giggled.

"Willow was as indifferent about having been away as I was excited to have her return. She looked in perfect condition and was completely relaxed. After she had put up with me lavishing attention on her for a while, she strolled off and carried on with her routine as if she'd never been gone."

I finished my tea and cake, reflecting on the incident as I did so. Then, continuing the story, I related, "When I told my cat-loving friend about Willow's reappearance, and the fact she acted like she'd never left, she explained, 'A cat's ability to mysteriously appear and disappear is something familiar to all cat people. It's part of their mystique.' My friend also told me that cats are telepathic to the point that vets warn people to lock them up on the day of a veterinary appointment, because they *know*. I have a hunch that their reputation for being mysterious is because of their association with Egypt."

"You mean the Sphinx?" Mariette asked.

"Yes. And come to think of it, I have a cat Sphinx story—though I think it's too early to tell that one."

"Oh, so are you lining them up now?" Mariette suggested playfully. "Michael Brown, are you trying to keep me alive?"

I smiled. "At least until Christmas."

"Deal," she said, pulling her blanket up over her

chest. "Now I feel cold again," she muttered to herself.

"Can I pour you another cup of tea, just to hold?" I suggested.

"No, I'll do that," she responded. "It looks like you could do with a refill too, and more cake." I got up and placed my cup and plate on her bed tray. It then occurred to me that this hospital bed tray, which bridged right over the bed and ran on four wheels, had in recent days become Mariette's whole life. On it she had a small vase of flowers, a picture of Pete and herself in a gold frame, and a notepad with a pen slipped into its spiral binding. All of this was neatly arranged on a knitted and lace-trimmed cloth on which appeared to be written *Bless All In This Home*. As I squinted trying to read it, Mariette remarked, "Pete bought this for me at Vroutjie Se Koutjie." She touched it gently with the tip of her fingers, as if it magically reached into a past now gone. "It's just a little something from my home. It hung in the hall."

As she poured the tea, she said, "I'm curious. Have you ever been able to communicate telepathically with your cats?"

"One thing I've noticed is that, even after being around cats for so many years, I can't *make* telepathic encounters happen with them. However, one thing seldom fails—and maybe this is a clue to why, when I try too hard, it doesn't happen. If I wonder where a particular cat is—not because I'm worried or concerned, but just out of casual curiosity—within seconds that cat makes an appearance. Then next thing, it's rubbing itself against my leg."

"They pop through a portal," Mariette declared.

"They do," I agreed. "They come to mind quite spontaneously, and this instantly pulls them from wherever they are. It happens so often and so regularly that, to me, the telepathic connection is undeniable. Through this, they taught me something about how to communicate effectively with them—gently, lightly, and curiously."

"So what happened to Willow and Maya?"

At this, my body flushed hot and my face heated to the point I was almost sweating. For a moment, I realized I couldn't speak. Neither could I hide my discomfort.

"Did something bad happen to them?" Mariette inquired gently.

"*I* happened to them," I said sadly.

"What do you mean?"

"You know, Mariette, I don't know whether I want to tell that story. I haven't spoken about it to anyone, ever. For some it might not be a big thing, but for me it was the *worst* thing."

I had somehow hidden the memory of this event from myself, which meant I hadn't even considered that my enthusiastic storytelling might lead me right back into that moment. I suddenly felt cornered by my enthusiasm to tell these "cat stories," an enthusiasm that suddenly subsided. It was as if some part of me had *set me up*.

"Did you betray them?" Mariette asked unexpectedly.

"How did you know?" I said, surprised by her accuracy.

"Because I read a lot of books," she said, her tone kindly, "and in every good story the betrayal always comes early." She took a deep breath. "I'm tired anyway. I appreciated your stories today, Michael. They lift my spirits during my time here at the hospital."

As she reached out her hand, I rose and took it. She had mercifully given me a way out, and I was grateful to be able to make my getaway. "I'll see you when you feel ready to tell that part," she said softly.

I cried on my way home.

8

The Betrayal

DECEMBER 14TH

I had spent the previous evening not only thinking about what I was going to say to Mariette on my next visit, regarding Maya and Willow, but *how* I was going to say it. To resurrect such an issue initially felt horrible.

Whenever I experience such emotions, I sit with the feeling. As I did so that evening, I noticed I was actually no longer highly charged emotionally. In the past, I'd spent much time with that wound. Now, revisiting it, I discovered it was mostly healed. The real issue was no longer what had occurred, but the fact I had never shared it with anyone because I still felt ashamed.

Mariette was waiting for me in the garden, tea tray ready, but no cookies. My intuition had told me not to bring anything to eat either, and she appeared relieved. As she welcomed me, smiling, I thought she looked a little pale. However, she sounded excited as she announced, "I saw a cat this morning!"

"Really? Where?" Squeezing her hand gently, I sat down.

"Over there," she said, raising her arm just enough to point toward the far corner of the spekboom hedge. "You were right," she grinned.

"What do you mean?" I asked, puzzled.

"I tried to *telepathically* call it onto my lap, but it didn't so much as look this way."

"Ah." I smiled at the childlike enthusiasm that still inhabited an old body.

"Help yourself to tea," she invited.

I got up, poured my tea, and we remained silent until I was again seated. I could feel that, although she wasn't going to bring up the topic herself, Mariette was clearly waiting for me to talk about what I'd brought up the day before.

"Not *too* hot this morning," I said, taking my first sip of the refreshing brew. "The weather, I mean."

"Mm," she replied disinterestedly. A too-long silence ensued.

I finally blurted out defensively, "It's not a big deal. I don't know why I didn't want to talk about it. Well, I do, but that's of no consequence. I think I'd like to tell you about it."

Mariette perked up, now fully attentive and peering at me expectantly.

"I remember someone once saying to me that if they came back to earth for another life, they would want to come back as one of my cats," I began.

"I'm sure they would," she said with a chuckle.

"I guess I do put my cats before myself now. Somehow I sense that if I take care of them, I'll be taken care of. I certainly know that if they are happy, I'm happy. It was Willow and Maya who taught me this—the hard way, unfortunately. I discovered that if I let something bad happen to them, I would find it hard to forgive myself."

My voice was wavering as I spoke, so I paused to draw a deep breath before continuing, "Willow and Maya moved with me through about four homes, until I left South Africa in 1993. It's funny, but my departure had been predicted by a woman by the name of Jean Holland a decade earlier, while I was still at university. She thought of herself as a sort of "channel.""

"Fascinating stuff that," Mariette said. "Though Pete used to say it's not very Christian." She paused, evidently thinking back to conversations with her husband. Then, as if snapping back to the present, she inquired, "So, she told you that you would one day be leaving?"

"Yes, she described in detail the sudden arrival of a particular person in my life and the circumstances that would signal my departure. She said I would travel to America to gather information, the result of which would be that I would bring some important work into the world."

"And that turned out to be your books."

"I guess so."

"You really have had a blessed life."

"I know," I agreed, smiling.

"So, continue."

"Where was I?"

She smiled broadly. "You were in love."

"At first sight," I admitted. "I was making plans to leave South Africa and go to San Francisco."

"Exciting!" Mariette said, her face aglow.

"The one thing...." I hesitated. "The one thing I didn't make any plans for was Willow and Maya."

"What do you mean?" she asked, frowning a little now.

"It's not that I did nothing," I said defensively. "I mean, I did ask my cat-loving friend to look out for somewhere for them, or to take them herself if she could. But the fact is, for the most part I was completely occupied with the plans for my own departure, and of course being in love."

I felt emotion welling up in my throat and moistness seeping into my eyes. Nevertheless, taking a deep breath again, I plunged ahead. "The day before my departure, I still had no place for them to go. By now I was panicking, as you can imagine. I phoned my brother, and he said he would gladly take them. He had dogs in his house, but he assured me they were used to cats. My cats had never been around dogs before. If they saw a dog in the neighborhood, they ran from it."

"I'm sure they would adjust," Mariette said hopefully.

"Except that my brother's life was full," I continued. "He was expecting the arrival of his first child. He said 'yes' out of the kindness of his heart. Obviously I was relieved, since it gave me a way out of my predicament."

I took a sip of tea.

"The reality of what I was doing set in as I drove to my brother's house, with Willow and Maya crying in the car. The moment I stepped into his home, where a big Alsatian called Chaka was clearly running amok, I knew I was doing something truly terrible. I had brought my best friends to a place that, for them, could only be cat hell."

My chest heaved. Mariette looked at me sympathetically.

"As I put them in a side room and headed for the door to the house, a feeling of panic set in. Closing that door behind me with dogs jumping against it, I felt sick to my stomach. I said my goodbyes to my brother and drove away weeping. I knew I was sentencing my friends to a terrible fate, and that I alone was responsible. After all the love they had shared with me, I was betraying them."

Tears were streaming down my cheeks now, and I sobbed.

Mariette reached out, her hand clutching a neat wad of tissues. I took them gratefully, wiping my eyes and blowing my nose before continuing. "During my first week in San Francisco, I bounced back and forth between the excitement of being in a brand new world and the terrible betrayal I was responsible for in the world I'd left behind. I had sent two cats into a dog house—cats that had been my closest companions for four years, who had been with me through some of my most painful moments, who had sat by my side as I wrote my many articles."

I looked down at my feet. "In due course, I received the communication I was dreading. Willow and Maya had run away."

"Oh no," Mariette gasped. "That's so hard, because you just don't know what happened to them."

"It was a long time before I could even begin to forgive myself for such irresponsibility, and I probably still haven't fully. For years, in the early hours of the morning, I was haunted by my actions. When I first heard they had run away, my soul wanted to leave my body to go search for them. But I knew I had moved beyond fixing what I'd done. That's a terrible realization to arrive at—that the world in which I could have made amends to them had moved on, and I now lived in another world far away across the sea, with no way to take back the consequences of my self-absorbed insensitivity."

I blew my nose again.

"Those are big words," Mariette said softly. "What matters is what you learned from it," she added reassuringly. "I too have made mistakes that couldn't be rectified."

We both sat in silence for a few moments. Then a smile lit up her face, and she continued, "When you're as old as I am, you're sure to have made a few messes. I learned you can stay stuck from a mistake for a long time, or you can use it to become a better person. So tell me, what did betraying Willow and Maya teach you?"

"Like what you were just talking about," I sniffed, wiping my eyes again. "It's a painful lesson, but the fact is that some things that are broken can't be fixed. In time I also discovered that the presence of these mistakes in our lives serves a different purpose than that of something that has to be fixed. Because it leaves a stain on creation, the kind of selfish act I committed can never be undone. Nothing I can do could ever clean it off because it's become part of the fabric of creation. But this means it can also be revisited at any time, which brings up the need to learn to live with it. And, like you said, learn from it."

"So how did you—or I should say, how *do* you deal with it?"

"The only thing I can do now is treat the cats around me with the care and attention such divine companions deserve. As independent as they may be, if they live with me, they are souls in my care. That's a responsibility. Because of the many tears I've cried over my treatment of Willow and Maya, I've become more aware of how I act around *all* cats these days."

"I imagine this is why some people would want to

come back to this world as one of your cats," Mariette said with a wink.

Though sad, I smiled, and Mariette allowed the silence to simply be for a while before continuing, "You were young, in love, and your world was changing fast. In circumstances like these, we do stupid, even *foolish* things. But this doesn't make us bad people. It's what we do afterward that reveals whether we are good or bad. My Pete taught me that." She grinned. "Were I a cat, I would *definitely* want to live in your house."

"Thank you, Mariette," I said, not just relieved but grateful for feeling heard and in that way forgiven, even by myself.

After a few moments I continued, "Talking about Willow and Maya with you is the first time I've ever mentioned my betrayal to anyone. I guess I was just too ashamed. After hearing they had run away, I was haunted by not knowing what had happened to them. I used to have disturbing dreams of walking through a strange suburb in Johannesburg looking for them. Then I would wake up distraught."

"Wow, it really did upset you."

"It did. Then one night in my San Francisco apartment, I had that same dream—except this time a Native American came walking along the sidewalk of the road I was wandering down. 'What are you looking for?' he demanded, his voice stern. Dressed in a colorful shirt, blue jeans, and worn brown boots, he had long black hair tied back tightly in a ponytail that snaked down his back. In desperation I told him, 'I'm looking for my cats, Willow and Maya. They ran away.'"

"What did he say?" Mariette asked.

"In a deep, clear voice, he stated matter-of-factly, 'They are gone.' I naturally inquired, 'Where to?' His answer surprised me. 'Call them back to you,' he instructed. Then he strolled off down the road. When I shouted after him, 'How do I call them back?' he stopped and turned around. The next thing I knew, he was instantly standing right in front of me again. Whereas I had been on a San Francisco street, now I was suddenly in a semi-desert landscape. He explained, 'That's what you are doing now. Your heart is calling them back through sadness.'"

Mariette was riveted, so I continued, "I awoke that morning and soon the dream slipped beneath my daily activities. A few weeks later, my partner at the time arrived home with two black and white female kittens, each with a splash of white on the face and white-tipped tails."

"Really? Are you kidding me? Just like Willow and Maya."

"Yes, both black and white females, just like Willow and Maya. I was surprised when she presented them as 'our new kitties,' as she had made no real mention of getting any, though I knew she liked cats. It was decided their names would be Cleo and Bean. Cleo was slightly more reserved and contained, like Willow. Bean was a little needy, but more outgoing, like Maya. They loved each other, and they loved us."

"What a beautiful ending to that whole sad episode, Michael," Mariette said, glowing and looking relieved.

"It was healing to have them around," I agreed, "though at times they also triggered sadness in me."

"Did you acquire any more cats along the way?"

"I did, but only after we moved from San Francisco to Tucson. That was when Cleo and Bean got their first garden and became part of a larger family of cats. I rescued a few strays that showed up in the neighborhood."

Suddenly remembering a stray called Monster, I chuckled.

"Come now, share," Mariette demanded playfully.

"It's possibly the funniest cat story I know, but also quite sad in the end."

"Let's hear it then, sad or not. It appears to be today's theme."

9

Monster

If anything could shift my mood from sadness to laughter, it was recalling the story of a semi-friendly stray I met in Tucson that clearly believed herself to be a full-grown cougar. But how to tell her story? I had to think for several moments about where to begin.

"Okay," I dove in, "through the years, I have had wonderful encounters with stray cats, the first being that mother and her kittens when I was thirteen. I've observed how a feral cat's perception of you changes as it becomes tamed, from initially seeing you as another 'something to be circumvented' along its pathways through the neighborhood, to seeing you as someone familiar and recognizable."

"You mean it's like you go from being something to dart away from, to someone they stop and watch," Mariette interjected.

"Exactly," I confirmed. "The thing about being a completely wild stray cat is that no one has ever addressed *you* directly in any consistent way. Life to you as a stray is a stream of continually different things happening all around you, and you navigate these in the quest for shelter, food, mating, and having kittens. Then one day, on a route you've traveled hundreds of times, something calls out to you. At first you don't recognize it's doing so and naturally treat it as an obstacle to be bypassed as safely as possible. Consequently, you ignore it and go on your way. However, whenever you come to that same spot, the same thing calls to you, so you stop at a distance to see what it is. Cats are after all curious creatures."

Mariette nodded in agreement.

"While you're there, this thing calls out to you again, and maybe puts something on the ground before backing away to a comfortable distance. At first when it does this, you of course just *run*. The next time you come by, you anticipate this experience. Instead of fearing it so much, you find yourself increasingly curious. Checking out what has been put down, you discover it's food. Cautiously, you nibble on it, and it tastes good. As you're eating, the thing speaks to you again from nearby. Next time you're hungry, you come straight to this place. It's a pleasant environment, with no dogs, so you stay around for a while. After a few more visits, you finally decide not to leave. The next thing, you're running the show. You're stretched out or curled up on a comfortable couch, watching television, and being stroked and adored."

Mariette laughed.

"One such stray, which we met in Tucson, was a real character. My partner and I soon named her Monster. The name symbolized her larger than life 'furiosity,' if I might be permitted to coin a word. Monster sent every dog-walker running, regardless of the dog being walked. At one point during our stay in Tucson, we decided it might be a good idea to increase our income by renting out the cottage in our backyard. We had an immediate taker, a dancer called Dusty who called us from Las Vegas. 'The only thing,' Dusty explained to us on the phone, 'is that I have a dog that's *very* powerful and *really* aggressive, so I need my area of the yard to be well fenced off.' We assured Dusty that it was, and so she took the place."

"What happened?" Mariette asked.

"On the day she moved in, she drove up in her huge-wheeled 4 x 4 and proudly presented Tyson to us. He was indeed very big and raring to go for no reason at all, as many dogs are. 'This dog,' she oozed, 'can take on *any* dog and down it in thirty seconds flat. It's bred to fight and *win*.' It appeared from Dusty's tone that she was actually trying to intimidate us a little. You could say she was marking her territory."

I thought back to how my partner had glanced at me at the time, smiling knowingly as she realized I wouldn't be able to resist opening my mouth, and intuiting exactly what I was about to say. This crazy stripper from Las Vegas was actually delighting in telling us what an aggressive beast she was bringing into our midst, knowing we had only cats, like it was some kind of pissing contest.

When I shared this with Mariette, she urged, "Do tell! What *did* you say to her?"

"The whole thing was quite comical," I recalled. "Trying hard not to smile, I interjected, 'We have a cat we need to warn you about.' Of course, the young woman burst into hugely exaggerated laughter. '*A cat!*' Dusty exclaimed, shaking her head, also with considerable exaggeration. 'Yes,' I continued politely, speaking softly and calmly. 'She's called Monster. There's never been a dog that hasn't run away from her, so we hope she won't be a problem for Tyson.'"

Mariette laughed. "How did she take it?"

"For a moment she just looked at us, stone-faced. Finally she said, 'You're joking, right?' I looked across at my partner, who was trying hard not to smile. 'Look,' Dusty said disbelievingly, '*Tyson isn't called Tyson for no reason.*' The sarcasm in her tone didn't escape us."

"And was she right?"

"Tyson was indeed a huge muscle-bound bullmastiff with a spit-dripping mouth, lunging on the leash to go piss on everything in sight. It was my partner who spoke next. 'Well, just in case,' she advised Dusty, 'please keep him locked up, and hopefully Monster won't bother him.'"

Mariette was clearly enjoying the irony of it all.

"Visibly annoyed, our new tenant mumbled

something under her breath and, with Tyson dragging her along the driveway, bolted him behind the gate. When she returned, intent on unpacking her things, she instead started chatting with us on the front porch, telling us about her career as a dancer and how good she was. In the middle of her really boring monologue, a terrible yowling erupted from the backyard. Jumping up, we all raced around the side of the house. Of course, my partner and I already knew what had happened, having recognized the familiar sound."

"Oh dear," Mariette sighed, "I think I know what's coming."

"As we rounded the corner, there was Tyson cowering like a terrified puppy, his face already bleeding, with Monster hovering in front of him, up on her back legs, sort of like a cobra, continuing to lunge at him, her front claws extended and her vocal cords producing a terrifying screeching. The sound she made was disorientating enough. Add to that the poor dog's desperate yelps."

"That must have been so funny," Mariette giggled.

"It was, although it got even funnier. Before we could reach them, Monster leapt onto Tyson's head, clamping onto him with all her claws and biting down hard on his skull."

"Oh, my goodness!"

"I know," I laughed. "It's the first time I ever thought a dog was going to pass out. As we closed in, all of us shouting, Monster leapt onto a nearby garden wall, where she contently gave herself a post-skirmish grooming."

"And what happened to Tyson?"

"Once freed, Tyson first walked around in circles, moaning and shaking his head, almost losing his balance and falling over. Then, suddenly regaining full consciousness, he fled back into the still-open 4 x 4 truck and wouldn't come out again."

"You mean the dancer had to leave?"

"She did, thank goodness. She couldn't even speak to us after this. It was actually quite sad to see someone so mortified, and she left without saying a word. There was really nothing more to be said. Of course, I wanted to say, '*Well, that's why Monster is called Monster.*'"

"But I'm guessing you didn't have the heart."

"No—although my partner and I couldn't wait to go inside so we could laugh hysterically, which we did for quite some time. I laughed so hard as we rolled over and over on the lounge carpet that I thought I was going to need a hernia operation."

"That's a hilarious story," Mariette chuckled. "Monster must have been another one of those black cats."

"Yes, she was indeed. For a long time after that, I couldn't look at Monster without bursting into laughter. But as much as Monster gave us an experience of supreme comedy, she also brought me a sad moment. I mean, I didn't really know her that well, given that she was around at times, then not for days or weeks.

I think it was her fierceness I so admired. She never allowed any potential victim to find out who was the most afraid of the two, because she always attacked without warning and without restraint until the deed was done. Though I did see her have a skirmish with a cat or two, it was dogs she most hated, *any* and *all* dogs. As they and their unsuspecting walkers approached, she would find the closest ambush spot and wait, her haunches raised, locked, and loaded, the end of her tail flicking side to side like an antagonized cobra's tongue. The moment the dog came within range, she pounced, screeching, slashing, and always quickly dispatching both dog and human, who ran for dear life. It didn't take her even fifteen seconds, so that it was almost over before it started. We tried to warn oncoming walkers. 'Be careful, there's a stray cat over there that's going to hurt your dog badly,' we would shout. 'It's best you cross the street immediately!' But until you've met a really pissed-off cat, such a warning is meaningless to dog people."

"So did a dog eventually get Monster? Is that the sad bit?"

"No, it didn't happen like that. No dog could do that to Monster. What happened was that one day I came back from waiting tables and noticed Monster sitting quietly in the middle of the back lawn. That was somewhat unusual, but I made nothing of it. When she was still there and hadn't moved about three hours later, I went out to check she was okay. I discovered a docile, barely conscious, clearly dying cat. I rushed her to the vet, but it was too late. Monster had drunk a good dose of the luminous green antifreeze that drips from cars in the Tucson winter mornings. Apparently it has a sweet taste that cats like."

"How sad," Mariette said.

"The vet told me antifreeze kills the kidneys. I found the spot where she had licked it and cried my heart out for her."

I fell silent.

Reading my expression, Mariette sensed I had more to say about the incident. "What?" she pressed.

"I was just thinking about how important it is to remember."

"In what way do you mean?"

"Like Monster. She was just a wild cat who lived long ago in a suburb in a land far away across the sea. Yet by remembering her great fighting spirit, I give her life meaning, a place somewhere in creation. She's not forgotten. Her life meant something, to me anyway."

"And to Tyson," Mariette quipped.

"Yes, I'm sure it changed Tyson forever." We both laughed.

"Well, that's another beautiful story, Michael—just beautiful. I love these stories of yours. They make me feel as if I've had cats in my life." Then, sitting herself up slightly, she said, "I think that's enough for today." As usual, she reached out her hand. When I stood up to take it, it felt cold.

"Thank you, Mariette," I said softly.

She looked into my eyes for a moment and smiled. "You're welcome."

"Tomorrow then?" I offered.

"Tomorrow then," she confirmed as we gently squeezed hands.

"You want me to call a nurse?" I asked before departing.

"No," she said, "I'm going to rest here for a while. Don't worry. This is after all a hospital. In a moment someone will come looking to prod me with something."

10

The Cat Chief

DECEMBER 15TH

When I arrived for my Saturday visit, Mariette had guests. They were people I knew, but I didn't particularly feel like their company at this moment. Peeping through the doorway from behind their backs, I caught Mariette's attention, put my finger on my lips, and silently mouthed, "See you later." Without missing a beat in her conversation, she winked.

I decided to go for a late breakfast. It was at the cafe that I bumped into Lynn, the Aberdeen animal angel who ran the kennels on the edge of town. She was insect thin, but with a heart as big as the universe. Her days were spent taking care of rescues and looking after other people's pets while they were away. "I caught a whole litter of stray kittens this morning," she told me enthusiastically.

"How did you manage that?" I asked, curious about her method.

"I used a tin of tuna," she grinned proudly. "It works every time. One of the litter is tame, like it was raised by people. The rest are as wild as tigers." She laughed.

"*How* tame is it?" I asked.

Entering Mariette's hospital room a little later that day, I silently headed straight over to her. Sensing I was up to something, an inquiring expression appeared on her face as she asked, "What have you got there under your jacket? Chocolates?"

"No," I said, smiling. Hesitating a moment to heighten the suspense, I opened my jacket and plopped a sleepy white kitten onto the bed.

"Ag *moeder* [Oh *mother*]!" Mariette exclaimed. Then in a hushed whisper she inquired, "Where did you get it?"

"Lynn," I grinned. "She's yours for the duration of today's visit."

Just then there was a shuffling at the door. The next moment, a large nurse thundered from behind thick-rimmed glasses, "No pets allowed! I'm sorry, but you must take it out now, please. It's hospital policy."

"But what harm can it do?" I objected.

"It can cause infection."

Seeing the immediate disappointment creep across Mariette's face, I challenged bluntly, "You do understand that this woman is *dying*." This took the nurse aback. It obviously wasn't hospital policy to speak openly about death either.

Lowering her voice, as if not to let *death* hear we were talking about it, the nurse insisted, "I realize she's dying. That's why she mustn't catch an infection."

Mariette burst out laughing.

"What's so funny?" the nurse demanded, now visibly uncomfortable and sounding annoyed.

Mariette smiled kindly as she stated matter-of-factly, "What greater infection is there than death?"

The nurse just stood there, blank.

"It's okay, nurse," Mariette assured her. "We have no desire to cause any trouble for you. Michael will take the kitten out."

The nurse hesitated, glanced up and down the corridor, then stepped through the doorway a little way into the room. With a frown on her face and sounding stern, she inquired, "Can you keep it out of sight?"

"It appears to sleep all the time," I replied.

Peering at Mariette, she said in a firm voice, her tone reluctant, "Okay, madam, you can have it until *he* leaves." As she said this, she cast a disapproving look in my direction.

"We'll keep it well hidden," I assured her, "and I won't do it again, I promise." Giving me another blank stare, she turned, exited the room, and marched off down the corridor. "Thank you," I shouted after her.

Mariette carefully placed the kitten half under her bedcover and began stroking it. When she again looked up, her face alight with joy, her eyes were as bright as a child's. "You'll have to pour the tea today," she said, grinning. "I have my hands full right here with this beautiful little soul."

I did as told. For a while she oo'd and ah'd over the kitten. When she eventually looked up at me, it was to remark, "I had a strange dream last night."

"You did? What was it about?"

"*You* were in it," she said mischievously.

"I was?"

"Yes, and a Red Indian."

"They don't really call themselves Red Indians, Mariette," I informed her.

"Well, you know what I mean."

"What happened in your dream?" I asked.

"I can't remember really," she said, returning her attention to the kitten.

Once more we sat in silence while she lavished attention on her tiny visitor. After a while she looked up. "I remember once at the bowls club, you told Pete and me about doing ceremonies with the Indians."

"I remember that too," I said as the memory came flooding back.

"I was wondering, do you have any cat stories with you and Red Indians in them?"

"Native Americans," I corrected her.

"Ja, them. Do you have any cat stories about them?"

Mulling her question, I sipped my tea. As two different memories popped into my mind, I ventured, "Actually, I do."

Placing my teacup on the side table, I made myself comfortable. "By the time we had lived in Tucson for a couple of years," I began, "we had acquired two more cats. There was Pokkie, a shy female black cat with a little white marking on her nose. I don't remember much about her other than that she was sweet. Then there was Mr. Pickle, a beautiful white and grey male kitten with light blue eyes. My partner found him in the Tucson Botanical Gardens. It was the middle of summer, with the intense Arizona heat scorching the landscape."

"Oh, the poor thing," Mariette sympathized.

"When she brought him home and presented him to me, she explained, 'His name is Mr. Pickle—he told me this the moment I saw him. He also told me he was *very* thirsty.' Mr. Pickle turned out to be a perfect gentleman with comic alertness and a huge heart. He also grew *very* big. So now we had Cleo and Bean, Pokkie and Pickle, and Monster. There were other cats that came in and out of our house, though I don't recall their names."

"What were you doing in Tucson?"

"I was exploring self-healing, which I had begun before moving there. It was what I was interested in at the time. In San Francisco, I had studied Swedish massage and Reiki, but it was in Tucson that I discovered rebirthing."

"Massage I'm familiar with, but Reiki and rebirthing—what are they?"

"They are different healing techniques I was learning at the time. Reiki is like the laying on of hands, whereas rebirthing is a form of healing that uses our breathing."

"So you *are* a healer!"

"I'm not a healer at all," I countered. "I was just studying those things at the time because I was in a lot of pain. They also interested me. Back then, I confess I did open a healing practice. Like most people who start off trying to heal themselves, I became more interested in healing other people."

I paused to smile at myself.

"Is that how you met the...." She hesitated. "What did you call those natives?"

"Native Americans. And yes, it was through my healing practice in Tucson that I met a woman who took me to my first sweat lodge."

"And what's *that*?"

"It's a ceremony that Native Americans do for cleansing. They construct a rounded tent-type structure, built low to the ground and completely covered, so you have to crawl in. Then they bring in round volcanic rocks taken from a huge fire in which they've been made red-hot. Then they throw herbs, such as cedar and sage, onto the rocks, along with water to create steam."

"Like a nice-smelling sauna."

"Yes, like a nice-smelling sauna," I chuckled. "Except that, depending on who's running it, it can also be the hottest sauna you could ever imagine sitting in."

"I could use one of those some days," she said, adjusting her position beneath the blankets, "especially when I get the shivers."

"I imagine you could."

Getting up, I poured her another cup of hot tea and placed it in her hands. "Thank you," she said, smiling gratefully.

"It was while facilitating others that I was introduced to cats as healers," I explained as I sat myself back in my chair. "It's a role that's natural for them, and they appear to be quite committed to it. Over months of facilitating rebirthing, massage, and Reiki, it became obvious that certain cats gravitated to certain people. The synchronicity with which a cat showed up for a particular person became almost predictable. However, there was one client, a Native American named Jeff, on whom all the cats magnetically converged."

"Are you saying he was a cat magnet?"

"Precisely."

"Like you?"

"Oh, even more so! Whenever he arrived for his appointment, all the cats came and presented themselves to him, whereupon he lavished attention on each of them. One afternoon, after a session of rebirthing, he shared with me why he liked the breathing as a healing tool. 'It does the same thing for me as what happened on my vision quest,' he explained in his forthright manner."

"What's a vision quest?"

"It's also a Native American ceremony. They spend four days alone in the desert fasting and praying. Traditionally it was something Native American braves participated in around age 21, though these days there are a lot of people doing it at all ages. During this period of isolation, they open their heart to receive a vision from The Great Spirit. That's the Native American name for God."

I continued, "Anyway, Jeff told me, 'It was on my vision quest that I saw my life's purpose, which is to make amends for something I did in another life.' Then, stroking Cleo on his lap, he explained, 'These cats are what I'm here for. I live on a piece of land just on the edge of town, and I have over fifty cats living with me. They're all strays, but I feed them and keep the peace among them.'"

"Fifty cats, and he was able to keep the peace among them? How did he manage that?" Mariette asked.

"I asked him that very question. He told me, 'I'm their leader and they understand this.' Then he added proudly, 'I know all their names. It may sound strange to you, but The Great Spirit showed me that I was once a cat. In fact, I was the leader of a large cat clan, but I let them down badly. Now I make amends by taking care of the cats who no longer know how to live as a clan.' Naturally, I couldn't help but flash back to my irresponsibility around Willow and Maya. Jeff's words got me wondering whether there might be some way for me not just to live with what I'd done, but to show caring in a manner that would make amends."

"Maybe there will," Mariette said. "What fascinates me is the way Jeff didn't have to go looking for this job. You mentioned earlier that cats just converged on him."

"Yes, as you put it, he was a natural cat magnet," I confirmed. "In fact, acknowledging the obvious gathering of cats at his feet, he told me one day, 'All cats know me. To them I'm a big Cat Chief.' He laughed as he said this, though I could tell he was proud of his role. Then he became serious again. 'It's my destiny to take care of them, and I accept it. You see, people think it's *they* who have domesticated the cat, but for the most part it's the other way around.'"

I thought for a moment before continuing. How much should I share about the history of cats? Would Mariette find it fascinating as I did, or was she too tired for such detail? I decided to give it a try.

"Jeff went on to relate how, because of The Sphinx, people think cats were first domesticated around 4,000 years ago in Egypt. But he said they weren't. He explained how their domestication actually stretches back to the beginning of our most recent age, which started in Turkey 10,000 years ago. He believed that a cat's spirit isn't even from this planet, and he insisted that all his people knew this. They believed that a cat's body is like a physical antenna—the sort used to receive and transmit radio and television waves—for what he called The Star Nation. This is a group of beings who live in a star system Native Americans call The Seven Sisters. It's the reason this particular star system, also known as The Pleiades, is so important to their people."

Mariette's jaw dropped and her eyes became big like saucers. "How absolutely fascinating! Did he say anything more?"

"Yes. He went on to explain, 'Cats help humans more than we may know.' After he said this, he gently placed Cleo on the ground, stood up, and stretched, which is what he always did when he was about to leave. I stood to walk out with him. 'You know,' he continued, 'there was one time in the 13th century when the pope of the time, Gregory IX, decided that all cats should be killed because he believed they were used by witches and Satanists. So everyone began attacking cats, causing hundreds of years of cat genocide. Cats were tortured, drowned, stoned to death, and burnt alive.'"

"That's terrible," Mariette said, her voice a mere whisper. "Is that why cats are sometimes associated with witches?"

"Apparently, Jeff said the cat almost became extinct in parts of Europe. Of course, with no cats around, there was a massive rat infestation. The result was The Black Death, which wiped out a quarter of Europe's population. It was a terrible time, and a terrible death. As Jeff put it, 'Cats aren't just pets—they are helpers and healers. Plus, they deal with the rats! This is why I'm okay with dedicating my life to taking care of them.' With that, Jeff climbed into his large pickup and went on his way. And that, Mariette," I smiled, "is my first Native American cat story."

She looked up from the furry white bundle. "You mentioned the Sphinx again," she said. "Is it time to tell that one yet?"

"Well," I said playfully, "I *could* tell that one now, but it might be better if we do the other Native American story first."

"Okay," she agreed, nestling back in her bed. "Tell me that one then."

11

Play of Life

"This story took place a few months after I first went to a sweat lodge ceremony," I began. "It was the sweat lodge that started me on a path of participating in many other ceremonies, which is a whole other story by itself. But let's stick with cats."

Mariette nodded her agreement.

"The main type of ceremony I attended was an all-nighter conducted by The Native American Church. This story takes place after one of those all-night ceremonies. It happened mid-morning when a pleasantly tired and reflective group of us sat under the gazebo, which thankfully provided us with shade from the baking sun. In the midst of us, lying stretched out on the shaded earth, was a Native American called Colin Kingfisher, now the late Colin Kingfisher. He was a Cheyenne elder, Cheyenne being the tribe he was born into, and he conducted the ceremony we had just completed. It was the first time he had visited the ceremonial grounds we used, which were at a place called The Peyote Foundation."

"What's peyote?" Mariette quizzed.

"It's a small cactus that grows mainly in Mexico and in some parts of Texas. It's used by the Native American Church as a sacrament."

She made a face. "You mean they eat it?"

"They do."

"I've eaten raw Aloe Vera and that tasted disgusting," she chuckled. "I took it for my stomach one time, but *never* again."

I smiled. "I've also tasted raw Aloe, and I can tell you that the taste of peyote is a thousand times worse."

She shook her head. "Then why do they eat it?"

"Because the effect of eating the plant puts them in the spiritual state they like to be in when they pray to and praise The Great Spirit."

"I see."

"So there Kingfisher lay on the ground in the gazebo, on his side, his head propped up by one hand, and in the other a rattle. '*Yo wanna heyona, Yo wanna heyona, Yo wanna heyona, Hey nay yo way,*' he sang, his voice soft."

"That's very good," she said, sounding surprised. "You can sing their songs!"

"I can," I said, grinning. "The songs I learned in those ceremonies are some of my most precious treasures."

"Sing another," she urged, "then you can carry on with the story. Please man, Michael! I never heard such a thing before."

"Okay," I agreed reluctantly. "A short one. This is a Kingfisher song. *Ah ha ha neyo, Janna wanna heyo neyo, Weya heyona hey nay, Janne wanna heyo neyo, Weya heyo neyo, Janna wanna heyo neyo, Weha heyona hey nay yo way.*"

I stopped singing. Mariette sat still for a moment, eyeing me intently, her eyes moist. "That's so beautiful, Michael," she said at last. "It reminds me of something, but I can't remember what."

"My whole time doing ceremony with Native Americans was like that," I said.

"How absolutely marvelous," she replied.

"So on with the story. There was King, as we all called him, spread relaxed on the gazebo floor, singing softly. We all knew this particular song because it was a favorite, the one he always taught people first and also the easiest to learn. Normally when King started shaking his gourd and sang, we spontaneously sang along with him. However, there was something about his singing this particular morning that turned us into quiet listeners. Aware he had our full attention, he stopped singing, put down his gourd, and slowly and deliberately selected a few pebbles from the ground around him. Once he had accumulated a small pile, he looked over very deliberately toward a nearby patch of long dried desert grass. As we naturally followed his eyes, we noticed three young kittens playing pounce-and-catch with each other. Meticulously selecting one of his pebbles, King threw it into the long dried grass, just close enough to the kittens to capture their attention. Of course, the kittens instantly stopped their play and, curious about what caused the noise in the grass, moved in the direction of the pebble. At first they were cautious, then began stalking, and finally pounced playfully on the spot from which the sound of the pebble landing had come."

Mariette looked up from the kitten she was stroking and smiled broadly. It was clear she was enjoying every moment of the story. Her response drew me even deeper into revealing the beautiful memory.

"King then selected another pebble and carefully landed it a few feet away. This again drew the kittens' attention. We all laughed, but not just at the kittens. We were enjoying King's playfulness as he continued to send the kittens in whatever direction he chose. Once he had depleted his stock of pebbles, save for one lone pebble, he lay back down outstretched, his head again cupped in his hand, his gourd in shaking position. After rattling the gourd for a few seconds, he smiled at us. 'Those kittens are funny,' he said, grinning. 'They imagine they are chasing a creature of some sort, such as a mouse or rat, when there's nothing of the kind there at all. As long as you keep throwing stones, they'll continue running toward where the sound comes from.' He shook his gourd again for just a moment, then looked up at us. 'The strange thing is, the kittens never stop to ask who's throwing the pebbles.'"

"How interesting," Mariette exclaimed. "It's so

true. They have no idea of where the stones are coming from."

"That is exactly what King was trying to bring to our attention—that the kittens chase the sound and nothing more. When they get there, they find nothing but a stone each time. I remember how King chuckled to himself when he declared, 'We humans are just the same. All day long we chase the sound of our own thoughts. But no matter how much we chase them, they lead us nowhere.'"

I sat forward in my chair. "It's what King said next that really stuck with me."

"What was that?" Mariette pressed, looking up from her furry bundle again.

"He said, 'We never stop to ask, Is this *my* thinking? Are these *my* thoughts?' Then he pointed out how we're so busy chasing our thoughts that we don't notice the feelings that are actually driving these thoughts. We don't recognize that the noise that causes us to pounce and pounce and pounce, each time finding nothing, is coming from our heart."

Mariette shook her head, visibly moved by the insight. "Wow. I hadn't thought of it like that—that our thinking is being driven by our feelings."

"There's more. King rattled his gourd again for a few seconds, then informed us, 'Only when we stop chasing our thoughts can we recognize that the heart is behind it all. And only then can we ask the question, Who's putting this feeling in my heart? If we don't get to the place where we ask *that* question, we may live our whole life jumping playfully after stones in the grass—and like the kittens, we may just be playing our life in *someone else's* game.'"

"Wow," Mariette exclaimed. "I think that's what I've been doing most of my life."

"At this point," I continued, "King reached for his last pebble, flicking it into the long grass, and the kittens predictably stalked it and pounced on it. 'The heart of the matter is more often than not a matter of the heart,' King concluded, resuming his gourd playing and singing, '*Yo wanna heyona, Yo wanna heyona.*' As the kittens continued to explore the long grass, we joined in the singing this time, serenading the gift of the morning's insight together."

I sat back and looked at Mariette.

"*Another* beautiful story," she said, clearly delighted, "and such a lesson in it." Then, becoming reflective, she said quietly, "You've really given me something to think about today, Michael. I've heard it said that our thoughts are in many cases what cause us so much heartache. Doctor Olive told me this soon after Pete died. She said I was to watch my thinking and not let it get me so upset. She said we often tell ourselves things that unnecessarily cause us fear, anger, jealousy—all those sorts of upsetting feelings."

Falling silent, contemplating, she finally concluded, "I just never considered that it's actually our heart, our feelings, that are troubling us behind our thinking."

"I can tell you, it gave me something to think about at the time," I agreed. "And now that I think about it again, that moment may have been one of the seeds that grew into my first book."

"You haven't told me anything about your books," she noted. "I just know you write books."

"You never asked."

"Tell me now, then. What stories do you write?"

"I don't write stories, Mariette. Well, I guess I do, but the two books that are published aren't stories."

The white kitten I had snuck into Mariette's room appeared to be fast asleep, part under the covers and part out. Being careful not to disturb it, Mariette slowly sat herself up and motioned me to hand her my cup and saucer. I obliged.

"So what are your books about?"

"In a sentence or two, they contain the insights that came to me while I was exploring all those healing techniques, as well as what I learned from my experiences in ceremony with Native Americans. The first book offers a procedure I developed that enables us to revisit emotional hurt from our childhood, so that we can digest it and stop it from giving us indigestion during our adult life. The second is about finding peace within ourselves despite what may be happening around us in the world."

Mariette began pouring our tea. "Well," she said, as if speaking to herself, "I could have used those books a long time ago."

Once our teacups had been replenished, she looked at me quizzically. "So you *are* a healer then."

"No, if anything I'm a self-healer, and even at that I'm shockingly bad."

"You give yourself no credit, Michael. You do realize that, right?"

I smiled sheepishly. "I've been told that before."

"So," she said, "did you ever get healed by one of your cats?"

"I'm sure I'm healed by them daily in many ways I don't even recognize."

Her tone turned mischievous. "There must be a story in there somewhere."

Sipping my tea, I scanned my memories. "You know," I said after several moments, "there *is* one that I recall."

She smiled. "I'm sure we have time for one more," she said, nestling into her bed, "then the kitty can stay here with me just a little longer." Being careful not to disturb the furry bundle on her lap, she made herself comfortable, then looked at me expectantly.

12

Anger Kills

"This story happened just shortly after I completed a four-day experience, a kind of vision quest in which I discovered the extent of my own pent-up rage."

"You did a vision quest?"

"It wasn't a Native American vision quest," I explained. "It was more like something I was facilitated through to help me see myself in a way I hadn't been able to. Up to that point in my life, I considered myself to be a *very* nice person. But through this four-day experience, I discovered my 'nice' behavior was just a mask. Underneath it I was actually an angry person. I realized that much of my niceness was fake, and that I was really being nice only to avoid getting into conflict. I didn't yet know the difference between being nice and being kind."

"My husband used to say the same thing about me," Mariette said. "He claimed I was the angriest person he knew who never got angry." She sat in silence for several moments, reflecting. Then she asked, "Do you think this is why I got cancer?"

"I don't know, Mariette," I replied. "Only you can know whether that's the case."

"I guess you're right about that," she agreed, lapsing back into silence as if she was scanning herself inwardly. Looking up at me, she asked, "When you found out how angry you were, did you change?"

"Not straight away. Besides, I'm still angry."

We both laughed.

"The problem was that once I had been introduced to my own inner venom, I was unable to put the rabbit back in the hat. All day long and all through the night, I felt the energy of years of pent-up anger trapped in my muscles. At moments it was as if I was being wrung out—you know, like you do with a big wet towel before hanging it up."

Mariette nodded. "I know the feeling."

"It seemed everybody and everything annoyed me, and it took all my focus to stop myself from verbally ripping people's heads off."

"I can't imagine you so angry," she said, shaking her head.

"I'll tell you one thing, Mariette," I chuckled. "Seeing as I was earning my living waiting tables, this wasn't a good state to be in."

"I'm sure," she agreed.

"By the end of each day, I was a cauldron of fury. When I arrived home from my shift, I knew that if I didn't let it out, I would hurt myself or lose my temper and hurt someone else. I felt I might even die."

"It sounds like you were in quite a bad way," she sympathized.

"I really was. I felt as if I had absolutely no control over my emotions."

"What did you do?"

Remembering back brought a smile to my face. "In complete desperation, using carpeting and towels, I turned my walk-in closet into a soundproof room so I could go in there after work to shout and scream and bang things loudly."

Mariette again shook her head. "I never heard of anyone doing such a thing."

"Believe me, it was a first for me too," I chuckled. "I used this closet for about an hour after work each day, after which I showered, ate, and collapsed into a fitful sleep. When I look back at that period of my life, it appears ridiculous, even silly. But it wasn't. Doing that possibly saved my life. It definitely stopped me from doing something really stupid like hitting a rude client in the restaurant, which was so tempting at times."

I took a large gulp of tea. "We all think we want to know the truth about ourselves," I said in a lowered voice, "but sometimes the truth overwhelms us. I was completely emotionally overwhelmed. Each day, I deteriorated. I felt like I was plunging into a deep, dark pit from which there was no way out."

Mariette's expression was serious now. "Hmm," she responded.

"After my closet screaming session one evening, a female grey tabby showed up at my door. She lived two doors down the street with the people I was renting my studio apartment from. I had briefly met them and the tabby when I was moving in. Like with most cats, the tabby and I had instantly connected, although I hadn't seen her again until that particular evening. She sat at the door for a long time just watching me. Then, curious, she moved through my room and eventually lay down in my soundproof closet. I was pleased to have a visitor, and her beautiful quiet presence calmed me. However, I thought nothing more of it—until, that is, she began coming each night, usually a short while after I'd finished my screaming, each time settling down in my closet. She did that for about two weeks. Then one day she stopped coming altogether. Around the same time, I felt a surge of clarity and presence, like I had suddenly surfaced from having been sucked down for months."

Mariette sighed. "What a relief that must have been."

"Yes, it was. I also realized I needed to return to South Africa from the States. In fact, I acted on it immediately. Over the course of the next week, I finalized my plans, then went to my landlord two doors down to give my month's notice. 'Thanks for letting me stay in that studio when I needed a place,' I said gratefully. 'I'll miss your cat when I leave. She came to visit me for a while and was great company.' Their expressions instantly saddened. 'Her name was Misty, and we lost her just over a week ago,' they told me. They had come home one night to discover that she had collapsed. They rushed her to the vet, but he couldn't save her. Apparently she died of kidney failure, though the vet could find no reasonable explanation for it. 'Well,' I said quietly to myself, 'no one needs to explain to me what happened to that cat. Anger kills.'"

Mariette seemed distracted, as if introspective, and I suddenly felt uncomfortable, as if I'd said something I shouldn't. Looking directly into my eyes now, she confided, "I've enjoyed your visit so much today, Michael. You know how to keep me entertained. Your stories are not only a joy to listen to, but they're also moving. I so look forward to them, especially the insights they bring me."

She reached out her hand, her customary signal to say goodbye. Standing up and taking her hand, I said apologetically, "I hope I didn't upset you with anything I said."

"No." She smiled bravely. "It's just that I'm starting to realize that I have been extremely upset for a long, long time. I have been very, very angry too." The smile disappeared from her face. "I'm really starting to think that the reason I'm here in this hospital is that I never shouted enough." Then, as if speaking to herself, she said quietly, "My dear Pete was right all along."

I didn't know what to say.

"You know," she ventured after a few moments, "I too have a secret I've never told a soul, not even my Pete. But that isn't a subject for us, Michael—not today, anyway. You and me, we are talking about your cats." Her broad smile returned.

"You can tell me anything," I assured her. "I won't judge you."

"I know you won't," she said, squeezing my hand. "I'm just not sure whether I can share this with anyone, or if I even should." Then, with a wink, she added, "It might be one of those things we just have to take to our grave."

I winked back as I said, "Okay, you can tell me when you're ready."

When she didn't reply, I added, "I'll see you tomorrow then, at the same time?"

"I'm not going anywhere—yet." She grinned mischievously. "I'll be right here when you arrive." We squeezed hands again, and I turned to leave.

As I approached the doorway, her voice stopped me in my tracks. "Aren't you forgetting something?"

I turned around to see her pulling back the bedcover. There on the bed, curled up, was the tiny white kitten. "Oh," I blurted out, "I nearly forgot."

"You *did* forget," Mariette said playfully.

13

No Visitors Allowed

DECEMBER 16TH

As I strolled along the hospital corridor, I was stopped by the large nurse with thick glasses from the day before.

"Mrs. Van Wyk is not to have any visitors today," she announced. As she spoke, I couldn't help thinking that, when she looked directly at me, the thickness of her lenses caused her eyes to appear far too big for her head.

"Oh," I said, "but she's expecting me."

"Well, you can't see her," she said definitively. Then, placing her hands on her hips, she demanded accusingly, "What did you say to her yesterday?" Her eyes appeared to get even bigger.

"Why?" I asked. "What's wrong?"

"Mrs. Van Wyk became very upset after you left. She even screamed at *me*. Did you upset her?"

"No!"

"We cannot have people coming in here and upsetting the patients!" She peered at me, awaiting my response. No words came to mind. An awkward silence ensued. Glaring at me, the nurse finally broke the silence. "You can come back tomorrow. *If* she's feeling better, you can see her then."

As I drove away, I guessed that bringing a kitten into the hospital had won me no points. At the same time, I wondered whether I had indeed upset Mariette with what I'd said.

The following morning, the nurse again turned me away. I became even more concerned. Had I upset Mariette to a point she no longer welcomed my visits? There are few worse feelings than when you think you've done something wrong to someone, but you don't know what it is.

"The doctor said Mrs. Van Wyk can't have visitors today," the nurse explained matter-of-factly, this time without any sign of annoyance at me. "She really isn't feeling well. She said can you please come back tomorrow."

"Can I at least look in on her?" I inquired.

"No. She's sleeping now. You can come back tomorrow." She turned around, and so did I.

14

Presence

DECEMBER 18TH

Mariette Van Wyk sat upright in her bed, beaming. I had expected to find her looking ill, but this wasn't the case. There were even cookies with the tea. I was greatly relieved as, delighted to see me, she reached out her hand.

My eyes instantly fell on a plaster that both hid and secured the delivery needle for a drip. Seeing me look at it, she commented, "It's a dull pain, itching more than sore."

"I've had a few drips in my time," I replied. "I could never get used to the sensation of a needle in my vein."

"They say I'm not getting enough fluids." She giggled. "They want to keep me well hydrated until I die." I was glad to see her humor was still intact.

As I made myself comfortable, Mariette reached for the teapot and began pouring. Watching her, my thoughts turned to how it must feel to be confined to a hospital room, knowing you aren't going to leave the premises alive. Three weeks ago, this woman who had such a bright outlook on life went to sleep and woke up in the comfort of her home. Now she went to sleep and woke up in a hospital room that was far from the familiar coziness of one's own home. She had been stripped of her personal clothing, her makeup, her precious daily routines, and even simple things like being able to make a cup of tea the way she liked it. Yet she showed no outward fear of dying, and it occurred to me how brave she was.

After she had finished pouring the tea, she said apologetically, "Sorry you had to be sent away. I had a bad turn. But today is a good day, so let's enjoy our tea and cookies, and you can finish the story about the cats in your life."

"When I was unable to see you two days running, I was concerned," I confessed. Then, with a grin, I teased, "I thought you might be giving Christmas a miss this year."

"What?" she chuckled, adding a second spoonful of sugar to my tea. "You think I'm going to die before the end of your stories?"

She looked at me now, a warm expression on her face. "I had a good think, you know, about some things I haven't allowed myself to think about for years. It *really* upset me."

I listened attentively.

Suddenly giggling, she continued, "When the nurse

told me that getting upset wasn't good for me, I told her to...." She mouthed the words.

I dissolved into laughter.

"Pete would be turning in his grave," she added, smiling at the thought. "Anyway, that made me feel *much* better, even though I still wasn't feeling at all well. But now I *do* feel good, and I'm glad you're here so we can drink tea and I can enjoy your stories."

"I'm glad you are here too, Mariette."

"Thank you, Michael," she said, handing me a cup with a cookie on the saucer. Patting the bedspread with her hands, she continued, "So, last time you were here, you said you had made plans to return to South Africa. Did you come straight back?"

"Yes, I did, for about four or five months. Then I returned to the States. For the next five months or so, I stayed in a small desert town in Arizona called Cascabel, followed by wandering off to Mexico for three months. Then after 9/11, I returned to South Africa."

"That 9/11 was a thing, hey?" she said, her tone serious.

"It was indeed," I agreed.

"You've sure traveled a lot," she added. "You are very blessed."

"Actually, my traveling days had hardly begun," I said. "After I returned to South Africa, I wrote my first book. While in Mexico, I had seen a clear picture of the book I wanted to write. It took a while after arriving back in South Africa to find a home, which I did in a suburb in Triomf. The small house I moved into, with its garden, was the perfect spot in which to write, facilitate others in the Presence Process, and once again have two cats. Having cats around was essential in such an environment."

"Of course," she agreed.

"I was ready to write pretty much right after moving in, but I still wanted to do another year or two of facilitating people through the procedure I had developed. I also figured this would be how long it would take for me to write the book, which would give me the opportunity to include what I learned from the facilitating. As we already discussed, cats are born facilitators because they do nothing and yet we feel deeply moved by them. They always bring a calming, peaceful vibration to a house, which is the ideal atmosphere for the clients. This being said, I made no effort to go out and find some kittens, which is of course what I wanted—two black and white female kittens."

She smiled again. "You wanted Cleo and Bean back."

"Or Willow and Maya," I added with a chuckle.

"Yes, or Willow and Maya."

"Anyway, one morning just after visiting with my brother and his girlfriend, I decided to pop into their local shopping mall to do a thorough grocery shop before heading home. As I strolled through the crowded walkway, with stores on either side of me, I heard a kitten's desperate cry. As the group in front of me parted, my eyes fell upon a wire pet carrier that had been placed on a small table right in the center of the flow of foot traffic. Inside it was a lone, short-haired, tan kitten with nowhere to hide away from the hubbub."

"Shame," said Mariette.

"That's exactly what I thought. Cats need a place to escape when there's so much noise and chaos."

"What did you do?"

"I immediately stepped into the adjacent pet shop and asked how much they wanted for the kitten."

Evidently pleased, Mariette's face lit up. "Did you get it?"

"The man behind the counter informed me, 'It's a little boy.' He told me all the red ones were boys. 'I don't care what it is, and you obviously don't either by the way you put it out there fully exposed,' I said as calmly as possible under the circumstances. He remained unmoved. I paid for the kitten, as well as buying a cat box, bowl, food, and kitty litter, and headed home without any of the things I had initially come to shop for."

"But you didn't want a boy," Mariette noted.

"No, I didn't, but there I was with one squealing in the passenger seat next to me. Anyway, on arriving home, I was pleased to discover that the tan kitten was actually a little girl."

"A girl?"

"An anomaly, apparently."

"Is that a kind of breed?"

"No," I said with a chuckle. "An anomaly is an exception to the rule."

"Because she was red but a girl."

"Precisely."

"What did you name her?"

"I immediately named her Presence."

"That's a beautiful name."

"As was she. However, from the start, she was a little withdrawn and shy. She particularly hated loud noises. Any loud noise caused her to run for cover. I wouldn't be surprised if it was the result of trauma from that shopping center. Who knows how long she had been in that cage?"

"So did you get her a friend, another little girl?"

"I did get her a friend, but it was a little boy—a saint in a cat's body, who I named Simran."

"What does Simran mean?"

"It's like a silent prayer you say to yourself over and over."

"That's beautiful. I like your cat names. So, tell me about Simran."

15

Simran

"You know, Mariette," I began, "I have wracked my brain, but for some reason I can't remember where Simran came from. I know that soon after getting Presence, I made a deliberate attempt to find her a companion. Somehow I ended up with this small black and white boy."

I smiled, remembering.

"When I brought him home, I placed him on the chair on which Presence was sleeping. He immediately curled up next to her, cuddling up to her like he knew that's what he was supposed to do, and went to sleep. From the moment they awoke next to each other on that chair, they were inseparable, except of course when Simran went socializing or was out gathering disciples."

"Disciples?"

"Yes, he had followers, strange cats that would follow him around. Unlike other male cats I had known, he didn't mark any territory with his spray to keep other cats away. Instead, he wandered through other cats' territories bringing strays home with him."

Mariette chuckled. "So you suddenly had even more cats."

"Not really, because none of them ever stayed for more than a few moments. Males and females alike just quietly looked around, ate food of course, then left.

"When not facilitating, I spent all my time alone, but Simran never allowed me to sink into a feeling of loneliness. The moment any kind of sadness arose, he would start running around idiotically like a mad hatter. If I got up from wherever I was to play with him, he'd dash to the kitchen and stand at the top of the stairs that led down into the lounge. I was expected to attempt to kick a ball of rolled up paper past him. He was a spectacular goalkeeper, which meant I seldom got one past." I chuckled, thinking back. "If I ever got more than three shots past him, he called off the game and wandered away!"

"Sounds like he was wonderful."

"He was," I confirmed. But then I fell silent as I recalled his fate.

Taking her cue from my expression, Mariette inquired, "What happened to him?"

"Late one afternoon, about a year after he had joined Presence and me, I was sitting watching television. I suddenly heard a car screech right outside the house, after which it drove away. I knew immediately what had happened. I knew instantly in my bones that Simran was gone."

"How could you know that?"

"I don't know. It's like I saw exactly what happened without actually seeing anything. I knew he died instantly."

"What did you do?"

"The opposite of what one would expect. I sat in that chair for about an hour, unable to move. All through that hour, I had no doubt what I'd find once I ventured out. I think that, in my mind, I was trying to keep Simran from being dead for as long as possible."

Mariette reached for a tissue.

"As the last of the light was fading, I finally got up, fetched a clean towel, and walked up the driveway. Turning left, I went directly to where a dark shadow lay in the gutter. But when I looked down at the body, I was sure I was mistaken."

Mariette sounded hopeful. "It wasn't Simran?"

"It looked like him, but the body of the cat that lay before me was much bigger than I recalled him being. For a moment I was really uncertain. But as I picked up the deadweight and placed it on the towel, I knew it was him for sure. He had died on impact and been flung."

"Shame," Mariette sniffed, blowing her nose. "That's so sad."

"It was. When I got him inside into the light, it was definitely our Simran—although he still looked bigger than I remembered. I placed him on the floor in the kitchen where we had played soccer. Presence came over and examined him. She didn't appear to recognize him at all. She then strolled over and curled up on the exact chair on which she had been sleeping when he first arrived. She never again became close friends with another cat."

"You must have been heartbroken."

"I was saddened for days. I missed him dearly. I know Presence did too. The thing is, cats aren't stupid, and Simran definitely wasn't a fool. He knew that road better than I knew it myself. Being hit by a car just seemed too odd a thing to have happened. Yet despite not making sense, it happened—and I was left to wonder what he would have been like had he become fully grown."

Mariette blew her nose again, this time loudly. "Did you get another friend for Presence?"

"I did. I didn't want her growing up alone. In my experience, lone cats tend to be more withdrawn, and I like my cats to be social beings."

"Who came next?"

"A cat with many names," I said mysteriously.

"Oh, that sounds intriguing. Do tell!"

16

Harmony

I shared with Mariette how, after Simran left us, I was determined to find a friend for Presence. I let my clients know this, hoping someone would have a good recommendation. A kind elderly client named Ingrid suggested that instead of our breathing session that day, she would run me to a nearby rescue center for cats. She was confident I would find the perfect little kitten to join our household.

"And did you?" Mariette asked.

"As we entered the cat rescue center, I was overwhelmed by the number of cats walking around in one enclosed space," I related, remembering back. "It was a largish area with some fifty cats, all seeming to get along just fine. As I was taking in this spectacle, an overweight longhaired tortoiseshell made a beeline for me, her gaze fixed intently on me as she approached, talking to me incessantly until I picked her up. 'You're very friendly,' I said to her, 'but you look pregnant and grown up, and I'm looking for a kitten.'"

Mariette smiled. "She of course disagreed."

"She most certainly did. When I put her down, she continued to insist on getting my attention. That's when one of the rescue center attendants informed me, 'She's up for adoption. Her name is Dusty, because she likes rolling in sand and is usually a dust ball.'"

"But the name Dusty wasn't one you liked," Mariette guessed perceptively.

"Definitely not. I told the attendant, 'I'm not looking for a cat like her.' But the attendant kept talking, just like the cat at my feet. 'We adopted Dusty from the Jeppe's Police Station,' she explained. 'We estimate she's about two years old. She was a stray, and they said they all grew *very* fond of her. Apparently she likes checking people's bags, so they thought she fit right in. But when she became pregnant, they called us, explaining that they already had a dog squad and didn't need a whole cat unit.' The attendant laughed. 'Well, I'm actually looking for a *kitten*,' I explained, 'a friend for a cat I already have.'"

With a twinkle in her eyes, Mariette said, "But she wasn't listening to you."

"Neither was the tortoiseshell, which was now putting one of her paws on my shoe."

"Too cute," said Mariette, a big smile on her face.

"That was what the attendant thought, too. 'Oh *look*,' she said in a cutesy voice, 'she wants to go home with *you*.' I ignored the remark. 'We have decided we're going to let her give birth,' she went on, 'so you can bring her back for that, then fetch her again after we've weaned her kittens. You are welcome to take her right now,' she urged enthusiastically."

Not, I remember thinking to myself, and shared this with Mariette. "'Let me look around first,' I told the attendant, 'then I'll decide.' Ingrid and I, *and Dusty,* who kept up her chatter, walked around the enclosure inspecting all the available cats."

I paused to take a sip of my tea.

"Did you find what you wanted?"

"No. I was surprised actually, as there were so many cats. Not one even closely resembled what I wanted. I was quite disappointed when we left. 'How can there be so many cats and not the one I want?' I asked Ingrid as she drove us away. 'Well,' she said, 'maybe it's not about what cat *you* want. Maybe it's about *what cat wants to come live with you.*'"

"And you knew exactly what she had in mind—Dusty," Mariette surmised. "But you didn't like her?"

"That was the question Ingrid asked me after we were in the car. I explained that it wasn't that I didn't like Dusty, but that she was everything I wasn't looking for. As we drove away, she lit a cigarette. 'That might be true,' she puffed, 'but *you* are everything *she's* looking for.' A few miles later, we made a U-turn."

"You decided to get her," Mariette announced, sounding pleased. "I knew you would."

"It appears the woman working there did too. 'I knew you'd be back,' she said, laughing as we entered the office, followed of course by Dusty. 'How?' I asked.

Her answer was cute. 'Didn't you notice?' she said. 'Dusty's a speaking cat. She told me you were *the one*.'"

"Delightful."

"Of course, I didn't keep the name Dusty," I clarified, "but immediately changed it to Harmony. I named her that because of the mirroring patterns of light and dark fur on her body."

"Did she and Presence get along?"

"Not like Presence and Simran. They didn't play or sleep together. Harmony was as outgoing as Presence was withdrawn, which is likely why they didn't have much to do with each other. Whereas Presence chose specific moments to connect with me, Harmony seldom left my side. If I was cooking, she was in the kitchen. If I was writing, she was next to me on the desk. If I was gardening, she was observing each activity. If I was bathing, she was on the edge of the tub. And always, she had something to say about everything. Unlike Presence, though, she appeared to be insecure, which was so strange because in another way she appeared to be afraid of *nothing*. While Presence hid from the thunder, Harmony sat on the doorstep getting wet from the rain. I assumed it was from living on the streets for two years."

"She was a bit more like Maya and Bean."

"Now that you mention it, she was indeed."

"So it's like all those past cats coming back to you."

"Actually, at times I've entertained that notion because of their familiar mannerisms."

"Did Harmony have her kittens?"

"No, she didn't. Her early days with us weren't easy. Within a week she became visibly ill, so I phoned the rescue center and they told me to bring her in immediately. I left her there for observation. During her stay, they decided to abort the litter to save her life, as she had a high fever. When I returned to pick her up, she was visibly shaken."

As if remembering something, Mariette frowned.

"It took a long time to convince her she wasn't going to leave us again," I continued. "I could see in her eyes she was asking me *never* to take her back there. I think this is why, if I was around the house, she seldom let me out of her sight. And if I went out, I always got an earful when I returned. Anyway, we became a happy and harmonious family together. With Presence and Harmony around, the house became a beautiful space for writing and facilitating."

When Mariette appeared increasingly distracted, I inquired, "What's wrong?"

"I'm ready," she said, her tone hushed.

"For what?" I asked, shocked that she might mean she was ready to die.

"I'm ready to tell you my secret." She looked straight at me. "I'm just going to say it once," she said firmly, "then I don't want to speak of it ever again. But I need to tell it to someone."

"Understood," I said reassuringly.

Her eyes filled with tears, and for a moment she

couldn't speak as waves of emotion caused her to heave forward, sobbing. When she finally calmed herself, she dried her eyes, mopped her brow, and blew her nose loudly. Then, now calm, she looked up. "When I was thirteen, I got pregnant by my father. One night they took me to the town doctor for an abortion. I couldn't have any children after that."

Her tears began to roll again. I got up and stood next to her with my hand on her shoulder. "Thank you for telling me," I said comfortingly. I didn't know what else to say.

"So you see," she said, again blowing her nose loudly, "I can understand what Harmony was feeling." Motioning to me to sit, she continued, "Hey, what's done is done. I've struggled with this all these years, but there is nothing I can do about it." Then, forcing a smile, she concluded, "And so we just get on with it."

After sitting quietly for several moments, she patted the bed with her palms, as she often did, then asked, "Did you get any more cats after Harmony?"

"I did."

"Good," she smiled, appearing pleased to have something else to focus on. "Tell me about them."

Relaxing back into my chair, I began, "I remember one day consciously saying out loud to whoever might be listening, 'That's it, no more cats. This is perfect.' Of course, I was tempting fate."

Mariette grinned. "Another cat came along."

"Yes, another cat came along."

Adjusting her position so she was more comfortable, she urged, "Let's sneak in one more cat story for today then. Who is this one going to be about?"

"A cat called Little Guy."

17

Little Guy

"**O**ne icy winter Sunday evening," I began, "as I was watching a movie, done with my day's writing and wrapped up warm, it occurred to me I hadn't taken my daily walk. I walked every day, the exact same route. It had become a beloved routine. Walking and focusing on the book I was writing, I'd ask myself what I wanted the reader to feel like after they had read it. Then I held that feeling, sort of like a contemplation intended to lead to its manifestation. But on this particular day, I had stayed with the writing and skipped the walk, probably because it was so cold. 'No,' I said internally to the idea of walking as it popped into my head, 'I'm not walking now.' It was already dark, as well as cold. Besides, I was watching a great movie."

"Which movie was it?"

"I was watching the first Matrix movie again."

"I don't know that one. Anyway, carry on."

"The idea that I should go for a walk wouldn't leave me. It wouldn't allow me to enjoy the movie. At one point I realized that, for some reason unknown to me, I *had* to go for my walk. It was my intuition urging me, and I recognized this. The moment I stood up and started dressing for the chilly outdoors, I actually felt like going for a good stroll. But my sense was not to take my regular route, so I turned left instead of right and strolled through a less familiar part of town. After maybe twenty minutes, I turned in a direction I felt would lead back home. Sure enough, it brought me out near my house. I found myself at a main traffic junction with a church on the corner. As I watched the cars leaving after the evening service, I distinctly heard a cry from a kitten. Listening intently amid the sound of revving engines and passing traffic, I suddenly heard the kitten shout, *'Help me! Somebody please help me!'* It stopped me in my tracks."

"You mean like real words?"

"That's what they sounded like to me—real words. First there were clear, distressed words. Then when I listened intently, what I heard was a kitten squealing desperately somewhere out there in the dark. I immediately began moving toward the sound, and after much searching came to a storm drain. Stooping down to peer inside, I could just make out the small bundle from which the sound was coming. To reach in far enough to pull the little creature to arm's reach, I had to break a dead stick off a nearby tree. Even though I was wearing gloves, I remember how, because it was so cold that night, trying to break the stick off hurt my hands. But I was determined to get to that kitten.

When I was at last able to extract it, I discovered that it was tiny, black, grubby, and just weeks old. It was small enough to place in my jacket pocket, which is where it quietly stayed all the way home. When I got back to the house, I immediately ran a warm bath so I could clean it up. As I was doing so, it remained surprisingly calm for a cat in water. When the dirt came off, I saw that it was a white and grey male. It was also badly injured. There was blood in the water."

"Ag, shame."

"I know. The poor little guy looked like he had been to hell and back. The end of his tail was snapped, the back of his legs had long cuts on them, and it appeared his hips were damaged because he walked a little funny, kind of like John Wayne."

Mariette giggled. "The poor little thing."

"To the disgust of both Presence and Harmony, I placed him on the study carpet in front of a heater, where I did my writing. I also gave him water, food, and a scratch box. Harmony didn't object to the scratch box and promptly used it. However, she voiced her objection to 'that thing in *her* study' loudly and insistently. I immediately named him Little Guy."

"Cute."

"Little Guy basically lay still on that carpet in front of the heater for three days, getting up only to eat, drink, or use the litter box. On the morning of the fourth day after his arrival, I was awakened by him clawing his way clumsily up the side of my bed. He completely ignored the hissing from both Presence and Harmony, who eventually fled the bed in disgust. Once Little Guy had made it to the top, he nestled up against me and went straight to sleep. This remained his sleeping spot for many weeks."

"He was okay?"

"He made a remarkable recovery, though I still wanted him to be checked out. The vet told me, 'That broken piece of tail will fall off, so just leave it.' When he asked me how his bowel movements had been, I replied, 'Now that you ask, he does seem to struggle a bit.' He told me this was likely because his hips had been badly hurt, probably from being crushed. 'The bones aren't broken,' he assured me, 'but it may inhibit his ability to pass a stool.' Handing me a tube of paste, he said, 'I recommend you give this to him. Put a bit in his mouth twice a day. It will lubricate his bowel.' He explained that it was likely I would have to give Little Guy that ointment twice a day for the rest of his life. 'Other than that,' he told me confidently, 'he's going to be just fine.'"

Mariette sighed. "Ag moeder."

"I gave him that slimy paste for two days, then the next morning I said to him, 'Listen, Little Guy, you are just going to have to learn to poop properly without this yuk, because I don't like giving it to you, and you definitely don't like taking it.' That was the end of that. He never had another problem with anything like that." I sat back and smiled, pleased at the memory.

Mariette reached out her hand, explaining, "Well, Michael, I've so enjoyed today. But now I need to rest a while." As I got up to take her hand, she commented, "You are indeed blessed, you know that."

"I know," I smiled, squeezing her hand.

"I really do think I'd like to come back as one of your cats," she teased.

"Uh, not in this lifetime," I grinned. "I'm not getting any more cats this time around."

"Well then," she chuckled, "I might just come back *in* one of your cats."

"*In* one of them?" I questioned, genuinely puzzled by what she meant. "How would you accomplish that?"

"Through a—what did you call those things? Oh yes, *a portal*." She winked. "I'll use one of your cats as a portal."

"As long as you don't show up while I'm in the bathroom," I joked.

"Now, Mr. Brown, you *are* giving me ideas," she said playfully.

As I exited the hospital, I noticed I didn't feel uncomfortable in these surroundings anymore. 'I guess I don't really hate hospitals,' I said to myself as I stepped out into the baking late morning Karoo sun.

The first thing I did on arriving home, after greeting my cat clan, was to make a delicious cup of coffee. I do enjoy tea, especially in the evening, and sometimes Earl Grey when I go to The Padstal for breakfast, but the taste of that hospital tea needed to be cleansed with the 100% Arabica Cathy had gifted me.

I took my steaming black-and-white-striped mug into the garden, with Little Guy tagging along. He loves strolling with me in the garden, and I love watching him examine everything as if seeing it for the first time. Someone had loved this piece of land, an oasis in the desert, before me, and someone had loved it before them. They left a beautiful community of fruit and nut trees, along with an array of established herbs. I felt so privileged to have been blessed with such a beautiful home in The Karoo.

Such were the thoughts and reflections set in motion by my visit with Mariette. I felt pleasantly opened and filled by my encounters with her.

18

Leaving Again

DECEMBER 19TH

When I walked into Mariette's room and discovered a neatly made bed, I was taken aback. "Oh, no," I said. "I hope...." Then I fell silent.

Inquiring at the nurses' station about Mariette's whereabouts, I was told she was waiting for me under the mesquite tree. As I turned to walk away from the desk, I let out a huge sigh of relief.

As I approached the mesquite, I noticed that Mariette in fact appeared healthier than I'd seen her since I started visiting over a week ago. Could she be in remission?

"What a beautiful day," she said cheerfully with a big smile. As she reached out her hand for mine, we squeezed gently as was our custom, peering into each other's eyes. Then I sat down.

Evidently comfortable, happy, and at peace, Mariette leaned forward and started pouring the tea. This done, she wasted no time returning to her favorite topic. "So you had Presence and Harmony and Little Guy." It was obvious she hadn't missed a beat of our conversation the day before. "How long did they live with you?"

"Three years," I said.

She looked surprised. "What happened at the end of the three years?"

"What happened was that I got my book accepted for publication. The moment I heard the news, I knew everything was about to change again."

"How so?"

"Because when my book was published, my publisher asked me whether I was prepared to travel to introduce the procedure I describe in the book. Naturally, I said yes. It was something I knew I had to do. Thankfully, I had about three months notice between the publishing of the book and my first presentation of the work in Princeton, New Jersey. I realized I would be gone for a while, possibly a few years."

I got up, reaching for my teacup.

"So what did you do?"

"For one thing, I made sure that this time my cats were *very* well taken care of."

"You learned your lesson," Mariette declared.

"I definitely learned my lesson," I agreed.

Picking up her own teacup, she sat back in her squeaky wicker chair.

"What I did," I continued, "was offer my house, my facilitation practice, and the cats to a woman named Dot. She was someone who was intimately knowledgeable about the practice, having been one of the first people to start the ten-week procedure. She had also begun facilitating people herself. But most importantly, she adored *all* cats, mine especially."

"I'm so glad to hear that, Michael," Mariette said, beaming. "What a terrific solution."

"During the day, Dot worked as a personal assistant in a business," I explained. "Then on weekends she did housesitting for people who wanted someone to take care of their pets. She was perfectly positioned to take over my space and clients, and she did so eagerly. This helped me go on my way with considerable peace of mind. Of course, it still wasn't easy to say goodbye to Presence, Harmony, and Little Guy, even though they had someone wonderful to take care of them."

"You didn't think you were going to come back?"

"No—although I eventually did. About six months later, I had to return to South Africa for a few months while a work permit for the U.S. was finalized. While I waited, I stayed in the house with Dot. After much moaning on the part of Harmony, I was once again accepted by the three of them."

I fell silent for several moments. Eventually Mariette inquired, "What is it?"

"I just remembered something," I said. "During my stay with Dot, we were watching television one evening, when she asked me, 'Have you noticed anything strange as you sit here and watch television?' I inquired what she had in mind. 'There's a tiny little presence that runs in and out of the kitchen in the evenings,' she explained. She said she only ever caught a glimpse of it in the corner of her vision, usually as she was watching television. 'Now that you mention it,' I said, 'I realize I've seen it too, also while watching television. However, it actually started happening before I left.' With this mutual confirmation, it was agreed that we indeed had a little ghostly presence running in and out of the kitchen."

"Simran," Mariette whispered.

"You know," I said, surprised by her suggestion, "that possibility has never occurred to me before. Do you really think it could be Simran?"

"Maybe," she said. "Our priest once told us that sometimes people who die suddenly don't know they are dead, and this is what a ghost is. Maybe that's what happened to Simran."

"I wonder," I said thoughtfully.

"Okay, so moving forward, you obviously left again."

"I did. And by the time of my departure, I could see firsthand that Presence, Harmony, and Little Guy were in good hands. This allowed me to feel at peace about leaving a second time."

"Did you have your own cats again in America?"

"No, because I was constantly on the move. I had apartments, but not a home. Although I connected with cats wherever they showed up, I missed those three."

"I'm sure you did."

"It wasn't like I thought about them all the time, just every now and then. Also, about three or four times during those years, I had a dream that usually took place in the mornings. It always occurred after I had initially awakened, then gone back to sleep again. In my dream, I would be lying on the bed wherever I happened to be staying at the time, when Presence suddenly jumped up from my side and lay across my chest. Naturally, I was always so happy to see her, and so I stroked her. Then I would wake up. My hand was always on my chest, and I was tearful and heaving with sadness. After the third time I dreamt this, I became convinced Presence was visiting me somehow, calling me back even."

"Through *a portal*," Mariette said enthusiastically, winking as she did so.

"Quite possibly." I smiled at her obvious delight at being able to apply the word. "Anyway," I continued, "just before I returned to South Africa, I had this dream again and wondered whether something might actually be wrong. I contacted Dot, who said everything was okay. But I noticed she didn't sound happy."

Curious, Mariette pressed, "What was going on?"

"Dot had purchased the house in partnership with a friend, renovated the garage to turn it into a cottage, and then her friend had moved into the house and she into the cottage. She told me the cats couldn't understand why they weren't allowed into their own home, which they apparently weren't."

"Shame! They probably felt like they'd been thrown out."

"That's what I thought, and I felt for them because it must have been so confusing. Of course, there was nothing I could do, so I told Dot I'd call again when I returned to the country. First I needed to go to Mexico. But after a couple of weeks, I got bored there and returned to South Africa, eventually ending up in Aberdeen."

"Why on earth Aberdeen?"

"That was a question all the locals asked me when I first moved in," I chuckled. "They wanted to know why I would choose to come live in a place that was dusty, hot most of the year and cold the rest, and often windy. Above all, they seemed to delight in reminding me that it was most definitely 'in the middle of nowhere.' Let's face it, Aberdeen is a drive-by, small dusty town three hours from the nearest traffic light."

We both laughed.

"My standard reply," I continued, "has never changed. 'That's exactly why I like it here,' I tell everyone. 'It's quiet, and it's likely nothing much will ever happen here.'"

Mariette evidently thought this was funny, for she again dissolved into laughter.

"You are so right," she said with her hand over her mouth, "it's just like that."

When her laughter subsided, I continued my story. "People of course look at me curiously and shake their head, or just laugh," I said. "Actually, what happened was that when my mother decided to move here, I happened to be in the country at the time. I helped her drive here, and I remember taking note that the town was similar to places I enjoyed in Arizona. I wanted to live in the semi-desert and watch cactuses grow." I smiled as I thought back. "As it turned out, after I arrived here, I became busy making a life and never got around to making that phone call to Dot."

"Did you ever see your cats again?"

"Wait," I said, "we aren't quite there yet."

19

Chubbis Choppis

"It was August of 2008 when I moved to Aberdeen," I recalled. "There had been no rain for quite a while, and most people's conversations were about the drought. I'm sure you remember that."

"I do," Mariette said. "It was dusty and dry, and often just gusty. Even the bowls green was turning brown." Remembering back, she shook her head.

"Now I know firsthand about those wild, dusty August winds," I said, smiling. "Anyway, I stayed with my mother for about a month, then found a place to rent that had a small yard and was closer into town. Because I had no dogs, stray cats used my garden as a thoroughfare. Although I noticed them, I didn't connect with any of them. Then one day that all changed. It was a midsummer's day in December, with the heat of The Karoo bearing down on us mercilessly. I was standing on the porch, absentmindedly looking out along the street, when out of the dusty heat emerged a compact, exquisitely marked, fluffy little white and grey cat. As it tiptoed across the hot dusty road, I noticed that it had an empty to-go bag in its mouth."

"It must have been hungry."

"It was so beautiful, and unbelievably cute, with delicate grey stripes and Frank Sinatra-style blue eyes. 'Only a desperate cat would be out in the sun right now,' I remember thinking to myself. I watched as he went through the hole in my property wall. I knew exactly what route he was taking, so I walked quickly back into the house, through the kitchen—and there he was in the alleyway. He watched me cautiously, licking the paper as he did so. I left, returning a couple of minutes later with a bowl of water. Placing it nearby, I backed away, whereupon he cautiously ventured over to the bowl. He was obviously extremely thirsty because he drank for a long time."

"You probably saved his life," Mariette suggested.

"Possibly. It's a funny thing. I couldn't help noticing how content he looked, happy even. It was as if he was entirely unperturbed by his plight. At the same time, he was curiously chubby—like a chubby little chop, in fact—while also small in stature, likely because of a lack of nutrition as a kitten. 'You are definitely a Chubbis Choppis,' I said to him, and the name stuck. By the time I saw him in the alley again, I had purchased some kitty treats. This made him a lot more curious about me, and also about what was in 'that doorway,' the place the food came from. Over the next few days, he would come to the kitchen doorway and peak inside, then dart away. Then one day he just walked straight in, systematically inspected the whole house, found the couch, curled up on it, and went to sleep. Chubbis Choppis had moved in."

"You had your first cat in Aberdeen."

"I did. And now that I think about it, it was for Chubbis Choppis that I first did something I thought I would never do."

"What was that?"

"There were three fully grown strays in that area, and they were vicious. When Chubbis Choppis took up residence in this part of town, which they considered theirs, they objected vehemently and violently. They would deliberately ambush him, terrifying him, attacking him. One day I found him badly beaten and traumatized. One of his ears had been shredded, his eyes were glazed over, and his happy-go-lucky spirit had clearly been frightened out of him."

"Ag, shame man," Mariette said. "What did you do?"

"Over the next three days, I caught all three of those strays and drove them to the SPCA. I knew perfectly well that because they were adults in less than good condition, they would be put to sleep. It was then I realized that I didn't necessarily like *all* cats. Chubbis Choppis showed me this. There were now cats I was prepared to kill in order to protect mine. I was able to save them, but I was also able to murder them when needs must."

Mariette flinched at my bluntness. "But you had a good reason," she affirmed.

"I believed I did. I was protecting Chubbis Choppis."

"Yes, you were protecting Chubbis Choppis, and perhaps other cats also."

We sat in silence. After several moments, I found myself thinking about Mama Sita and Baba.

"There's actually more to the story of Chubbis Choppis," I said.

Mariette smiled, waving me to carry on.

20

Mama Sita & Baba

"**O**ne of the benefits of clearing those three strays from the neighborhood," I continued, "was that Chubbis Choppis brought his mother and his smaller sister, obviously from a litter that came after him, to meet me."

"Ag, sweet!" Mariette exclaimed.

"That they were," I said with a twinkle in my eye. "Mama Sita, which is what I named the mother, was a pure white cat—although when she first appeared, she was a tangled mat of dreadlocks, hissing wildly if I came anywhere near her. Despite this, a beautifully pure vibration emanated from her."

"Did you tame her?"

"I did—eventually. But it was she who really allowed me to do so," I chuckled.

"Tell me," Mariette said, her expression all curiosity.

"I began by sneaking up and gently tapping her on her shoulder as she ate, until she got used to it and stopped running away. During the next few weeks, I was able to get at and cut off one of her matted dread-locks at a time. By the time we had completed this procedure, she was tame enough to be introduced to brushing. In the weeks that followed, she revealed her beautiful white fur and became known as Mama Sita, The Queen of The Garden. She had the sweetest nature but chose to remain an outdoor cat. Her daughter, who I called Baba, remains to this day the most beautiful kitten I have ever seen. She was luminous white, with shades of grey, augmented with little dark brown stripes that highlight her shading. Her majestic coloring and radiant blue eyes entranced me every time she tagged along with mom for a visit to Chubbis Choppis' new home. I felt she was a nature spirit for sure."

"An angel!" Mariette suggested.

"Yes, an angel," I agreed. "Anyway, Chubbis Choppis adored them both and regularly left with them, usually returning hours later. They had a special place in the wall where they entered and exited the yard. I loved watching them come and go. They were such a happy family together. I was glad to be able to make a better life for them. I even got Mama Sita spayed, which enabled her to settle down more. I always felt safe when Mama Sita was sitting up on the roof or high in the mesquite tree watching over me while I was in the garden. She felt like a guardian angel. So it appeared I didn't have to do much to become surrounded by cats again. Chubbis Choppis enjoyed having the run of the house, and Mama Sita and Baba enjoyed having their own yard. I now had three cats around me, which felt perfect."

"But you said that before!" Mariette added playfully.

"I know," I smiled, "and we know what happened next."

"You better pass me your cup," she said, reaching out her hand. "I don't want the storyteller getting a thirsty throat."

21

Dream Calling

As I took my freshly poured cup of steaming tea and sat back down, I commented, "Remember I told you about that dream I had when I was traveling?"

"The one with Presence on your chest?" Mariette recalled, getting comfortable in her chair.

"Yes, that one. Well, one morning, about six months into my stay here in Aberdeen, it happened again. I got up early, went to the bathroom, but despite having a cup of coffee still felt weary. So I went back to bed. From the side of the bed, Presence appeared, clambering onto my chest. I was *so* glad to see her and stroked her. As I was wondering what she was doing here in Aberdeen, I awoke."

"What did you do?"

"The obvious thing. I phoned Dot later that morning. 'I'm so glad you finally called,' she said, sounding concerned. 'I have to move out of here soon because we've sold the house, and I don't know what to do with the cats. I've been so worried, because I can't take them with me to the place I'm moving.' Well, there was no hesitating. I knew exactly what I had to do. 'I'll cover the cost if you can drive them down,' I suggested. Within two weeks Dot arrived and opened two cat boxes in my living room, one containing Presence and the other Little Guy, who was now much bigger. Harmony had insisted on being on her lap during the trip."

"Did they like the house?"

"Presence immediately hid under a couch and stayed there for quite some time before coming out to inspect her new surroundings. Little Guy ran into the garden and lay under a bush until evening. Harmony, being who she was, strolled around as if she'd lived there forever. By evening, all three cats knew where everything was and settled into their new home."

"What about Chubbis Choppis?" Mariette inquired, sounding concerned.

"It was all a bit much for him, so he decided to move outside again with Mama Sita and Baba. So now I had two clans—the Johannesburg city cats, and the Aberdeen small town cats."

Mariette chuckled.

"The two groups didn't bother each other, but they let each other know they definitely had absolutely nothing in common," I continued. "So there we were, three and a half years after we parted, all back together."

I grinned as I thought back. "Cats don't forget, either. I bonded quickly with Presence and Harmony, but Little Guy remained aloof for weeks. Then one day, as if suddenly remembering who I was, he came running over to me and was his same old adorable Buddha-boy self. I changed his name to Big Guy, and often I call him Big Fish. Harmony also went through a name change. After spending more time with her, I decided she was actually a unique creature of her own species simply disguised as a cat. So I started calling her a 'Botjie.' Then one day I happened to refer to her as Mrs. Botjie, and that stuck."

"What about Chubbis Choppis? Did he ever come back into the house?"

"Chubbis Choppis still came into the house to visit, but he kept his distance from the other three. Mama Sita and her beautiful daughter also became tamer and tamer, spending more time in the yard and less wandering the neighborhood. For a few months we lived as one happy, though segregated, cat clan."

I stopped talking as the memory of a horrible afternoon suddenly surfaced. Picking up on my distracted expression, Mariette inquired, "Tell me. What happened?"

22

Disappearance and Death

"**O**ne night," I said, lowering my voice, "I awoke with a start, knowing something had happened to Baba kitty. I didn't know how I knew, but I knew the same way I did when Simran was run over. I felt she had been attacked by a dog. There was nothing I could do because I had no idea where to begin looking for her. All through the next day, I kept watch for the Aberdeen crew to come through their hole in the wall. My heart sank when only Mama Sita and Chubbis Choppis appeared. My suspicion was confirmed."

"Oh dear," Mariette said softly.

"I walked through the neighborhood to see if I could maybe find her, but the dusty roads of Aberdeen were empty of her beautiful presence. I peeked into open lots and yards, but there was no sign of Baba anywhere. I already knew she was gone. Then, when I got home, I felt her presence. It was strong, and it was by the kitchen door. I could have sworn she was there. But when I searched, there was no sign of her. That was when I cried over her loss. I was sure I had felt her spirit."

"And you had felt the exact moment of her departure," Mariette added.

"I did. After her disappearance, something about staying in that house felt less comfortable, though I couldn't put my finger on it. Then one Sunday afternoon about a week later, I returned from my walk to hear a panting coming from beneath the couch. The other four cats, who were also in the room, were behaving strangely, watching that area. To my surprise, I discovered Mama Sita lying there, breathing heavily, looking visibly traumatized and wet with what I instantly recognized as dog saliva. This was the first time she had ever come inside. I gently pulled her out from under the couch, only to discover she had been badly mauled. It felt surreal, because I knew Mama Sita to be too wise to be caught by any dog. Yet here she was, badly hurt and terribly shaken."

"What did you do?"

"I placed her in the spare room, then next morning took her to the vet. 'I'll do what I can,' he told me, 'but she's extremely weak and probably has internal damage.' He confirmed it was a dog attack, and that whichever dog got her, shook her around pretty badly, which is what likely caused most of the damage."

"Did she recover?"

"Mama Sita sat quietly in the place I made for her in the spare room for two days, neither eating nor drinking. She even had a visit from Chubbis Choppis every now and then. Then one morning, I found her lying on her side in the early morning sun. There was no question but that she was dying. Regretfully, I rushed her back to the vet. He put her on a drip and kept her under close observation, but that night he phoned and said they had lost her. He sounded as distraught as I felt. He's a cat person too, you see. 'I get too close to these animals far too quickly,' he told me. 'It's an occupational hazard in a profession like mine.'"

"Did you have to fetch her body?" Mariette asked.

"The vet explained that I didn't need to, since they were set up for these situations. But first thing in the morning, I drove over there anyway and brought back Mama Sita's frozen corpse wrapped in an old orange shawl. I buried her deep beneath the mesquite tree that had kept her claws neatly manicured."

"You mentioned you regretted taking her back to the vet. Why?"

"I'd rather she had died peacefully in the morning sun. I'm sure she would have preferred that too."

Mariette looked at me and smiled sweetly. "You gave her a good life while she was with you. She even came into your house for the very first time when she was dying."

My eyes moistened.

"It's strange how these animals touch us humans," Mariette added softly.

"It's because they get right into our heart," I sniffed.

Not for the first time during our visits, Mariette reached out with a wad of tissues.

"Thanks," I said, adding after a few moments of silence. "You know what was *really* heartbreaking? It was walking out into the yard and seeing Chubbis Choppis sitting by that hole in the wall waiting for Mama Sita and Baba. Seeing him waiting patiently there just melted me emotionally. He sat there, eyes fixed on that hole, at some point every day for nearly two weeks." I blew my nose, and a smile erupted across my face. "Then one day he stopped waiting and became his own little person, Chubbis Choppis, the happiest cat that has ever lived!"

"Ag now," Mariette sniffed. "Pass those tissues back to me. You're making me cry—again."

We both sat there for a moment, smiling and sniffing together.

"Cats," she said finally, blowing her nose.

"Yup," I agreed, blowing mine. "Cats indeed."

"Well," she said, "I think that's enough crying for today."

"I agree," I said with a chuckle, "quite enough."

She held out her hand. "I hope you have enough stories to keep me going until Christmas," she joked.

"I'm sure I do," I reassured her, squeezing her hand gently as usual.

23

Turning

DECEMBER 20TH

As I walked into the hospital, the large nurse with the unbelievably thick lenses was waiting for me once again. My mood sank as I saw the expression on her face. *Oh no,* I thought.

"I'm sorry to tell you, but Mrs. Van Wyk took a bad turn last night," she said sympathetically.

I said nothing.

"The night nurse found her unresponsive, and she's been that way ever since."

My heart sank. "But she was looking so good yesterday," I countered disbelievingly.

"The doctor said this sometimes happens before..." She didn't want to finish what she was about to say. I could see she was visibly upset by the occurrence, and this immediately softened my heart toward her. She had of course already spent much more time with

Mariette than I. In that moment she transformed from being a hospital official to being a comrade of the heart. Whatever was happening to Mariette, this nurse and I were in it together—her even more so than me.

"I'll come back tomorrow," I said with a note of certainty, no doubt reassuring myself that Mariette would indeed still be alive. "By the way, my name is Michael Brown." I reached out, and we finally officially met. Her hand was soft and warm, and her touch caring. I was suddenly so grateful these hands and the woman they belonged to were around Mariette at this time.

"I know," she smiled broadly. "My name is Nurse Thandokazi. If you leave your number with me, I'll call you the moment there's any change in her condition."

I received no call from her the rest of the day, though Vicky called to tell me she had heard from Joy that Mariette had taken a bad turn and "likely wouldn't last the night." She wanted to know if I had visited her yet, and I said yes, but gave no further details despite the fact she clearly wanted them. Mariette had fast gone from a woman I once played bowls with to a friend with whom I had shared an intimate secret, and who had in kind shared something deeply personal with me. We had become each other's confessors, and what we shared was precious and not grist for the town crier's repertoire. I now felt protective of Mariette and wanted her remaining experience to be honored, not gossiped around the town.

Before going to sleep, I lit a candle for Mariette in my garden chapel. As I did so, tears left my eyes for the earth beneath my feet. Who could have guessed I would be so deeply touched by reaching out to touch the life of another? Cathy's face appeared momentarily in my mind's eye, and she was smiling with approval.

The following day, I returned to find the situation unchanged. Then the day after that, they told me the good news that Mariette was awake. However, the doctor had forbidden her to have visitors for the next twenty-four hours.

"Tell her I'll see her tomorrow, then," I said to Nurse Thandokazi, this time unable to mask my disappointment. I not only wanted Mariette to hear the rest of my cat stories, I wanted to be able to tell them to her. As I made my way home, I mused at how revisiting these cat memories had affected me. By recalling all the lessons I had learned from my many experiences with these magnificent creatures, I was learning a whole new one—a lesson about the power of friendship in a time of need.

24

Cat Heaven

DECEMBER 23RD

"**Y**ou had me a bit worried," I admitted as I entered Mariette's room and took her hand. She smiled weakly. "They told me you shouldn't speak too much."

"Oh, they did, did they?" she said with a rasped whisper, her face alight with a grin. Then she declared in a more assertive tone, "I'm not dead *yet*." Indeed she wasn't, for she appeared even better groomed than usual today, with her hair tied up gorgeously in a bun. "That nurse helped me with it," she noted as she saw me examining it. "She's not so bad, you know."

"I know," I smiled, reflecting on how hanging around in this hospital had changed my mind about quite a few things. "It's cheating if you leave before Christmas—you know that," I joked. "We have a deal, remember?"

"The deal still stands, young man," she said, her voice

again a rasping whisper. She looked weak, but peaceful. "I'm okay, really," she said, adding with a wink, "never felt better, actually." I could almost believe her.

"Where did you go when you were unconscious?" I asked, curious. Then, jokingly, I inquired, "Did they turn you away from the white light?"

"That's *my* secret," she answered, not missing a beat.

Sitting down in my chair, I noticed there was no tea tray. In addition to the large display of cards from well-wishers and the many bouquets of flowers, the room now contained an array of hospital equipment. Along with the newly introduced heart monitor, there was an oxygen tank in the corner, with a mask resting beside Mariette's pillow.

"How does it end?" Mariette asked, her voice even weaker now. "Where have your experiences with cats brought you?"

"Since we first began talking about cats, I've had some time to think about that. As a cat family, we had one more move to make before we made it into cat heaven."

"Cat heaven." She repeated the words softly. "That sounds like a lovely place."

"Yes, the sort of place I've always wanted for my cats, where there's room to run wild, without dogs, and *lots* of mice."

"Not sure about the mice," Mariette giggled. "But please tell me about getting into cat heaven. I'm going to close my eyes while you talk, but I don't want you to think I'm asleep."

"It's okay if you sleep," I assured her.

"I won't," she whispered. Then, winking, she added, "There'll be plenty of time for that yet."

"Okay, let me see." I became quiet for a moment, considering where to pick up the cat tale. "After about three years in Aberdeen," I began, "we were strangely all moved into cat heaven. I say we were 'moved,' because at the time I had no intention of moving anywhere, even though I was unhappy in the house I was staying in. I lived right on the edge of Aberdeen's town center, on a route used daily by masses of rowdy school children. The house was also on a corner, and as these kids passed by on both sides of the house, twice daily during school term, it felt like they were walking right through my living room. All the cats were happy at this house, but I didn't feel they had enough garden—and they definitely had too much street for my liking. Also, with what happened with Baba, then Mama Sita—well, it just didn't feel like home anymore."

"I can certainly understand how you felt," Mariette whispered.

"One morning there was a knock at my door. When I opened it, a middle-aged woman and her daughter stood there. 'I'm sorry to bother you,' said the woman, 'but we are thinking of buying this house and would like to look around.' I invited them in. As they looked around, they oo'd and ah'd, finally declaring that they were *very* interested. I asked them to give me a couple of months' notice if they decided to purchase the house, so that I could find another rental. They agreed and went on their way. Two weeks later they knocked on the door again. 'We've bought the house and will be moving in at the end of July,' the woman announced proudly."

"What time of year was this?" Mariette asked, still keenly tracking with me despite her frailty.

"It was around March."

"So you had plenty of time to move."

"Yes, I did," I agreed. "Anyway, they came in and measured for cupboards and curtains, then left. The following morning, Mrs. Botjie awakened me early by walking across my chest to get from one side of the bed to the other. She never did this, always showing me courtesy by tiptoeing around my head. That usually woke me up anyway, as intended, though not so abruptly."

Mariette smiled, her eyes closed.

"'Mrs. Botjie!' I moaned, not at all impressed, and rolled over. A few moments later she did the same thing again, then again. 'Mrs. Botjie!' I grumbled at her, finally sitting up in bed. 'Why are you doing this?' She just sat there on the end of the bed looking at me. It was then that I recalled what had happened the day before—that the house had been sold. 'We need to find a new home,' I said to Mrs. Botjie. She meowed in full agreement."

"Cats know," Mariette whispered. "So what did you do about it?"

"I decided to start looking that very day, like I had a bee in my bonnet. There really was no rush, but my intuition said, 'Go.' First I decided to walk around the part of Aberdeen I'd prefer to live in, which was more toward the very edge of town. I strolled along the few roads where there are more trees and larger plots with bigger gardens."

"Over on the northeast side."

"Exactly. At one point I passed a residence that looked unique, and actually quite out of place in Aberdeen. It was a log cabin-like house with wooden front paneling. More like a cottage than a Karoo house. The property looked to be about a quarter of an acre, with big trees and open plots all around it. 'That's exactly what I'd like,' I thought to myself. 'That would be cat heaven for sure.'"

Mariette smiled.

"Then the thought occurred to me, 'These sorts of places are probably all taken.' So I continued my walk and thought no more of it. After looking at all there was to see along those roads, I went to speak to Connie, our resident realtor. 'The property market is terrible at the moment,' she told me. 'I have only two rentals I can show you at this time. The first is quite lovely, furnished and ready to let right now. The second is full of chickens, and the people are still in there, but it is for rent and they will move if someone takes it.'"

"I imagine you preferred the first one," Mariette said.

"Connie also thought I'd prefer the first one," I said, "but I told her I wanted to see the one with the chickens. 'Ja, I will take you there,' she agreed, 'but first let me show you the other one.' The 'other one' turned out to be a square block in a depressed-looking street across the road from an abandoned butchery. The furniture was 70s, well worn, and there was no garden to speak of."

"You *had* to have a garden," Mariette chimed in, her voice extremely soft.

"Of course. 'This is a *very* good deal,' the town realtor assured me enthusiastically. 'I understand,' I said, 'but I'd like to see the house with the chickens.' As we drove, she warned, 'Man, these people have let the chickens and ducks live *in the house with them*, so the place is bloody filthy. The garden's beautiful, though. He does that permaculture thing.' To my surprise, she drove me directly to the log cabin-looking house I had spotted earlier with the huge open space and big trees."

"Right to cat heaven," Mariette whispered.

"Yes—though Connie was right, the house was in an atrocious state. In fact, it looked a bit more like hell than heaven. At the same time, I knew it was nothing that couldn't be fixed with a thorough cleaning. Besides, the garden immediately stole my heart."

Mariette opened her eyes for a moment as, clearly

delighted, she remarked, "It was exactly the sort of place you wanted for yourself and your cats."

"It was—and the house needed my cats. These people had only ever had dogs, which meant mice were running amok *everywhere*. As I sat on the porch talking to the owners, I counted at least ten of them on the roof of a storage shed."

"Ag sis!" Mariette crumpled her face with playful disapproval.

"They told me that if I took the place right away, they would move immediately. They offered me the same rental price I was currently paying, so I couldn't believe my luck."

"I told you that you're blessed," Mariette whispered, keeping her eyes shut as she spoke.

"I know," I concurred, "and I really felt double-blessed when I found that place on my very first day of looking and had already made arrangements to move in by lunch time."

At this point in my visit with Mariette, I was craving a cup of tea. Talk and tea belong together, and it had become a central feature of our visits.

"Carry on," Mariette urged, her voice a bare whisper. "I want to hear the rest of this story."

"Within two weeks I was unpacking. And the cats were, as I knew they would be, in cat heaven."

"Aah, how wonderful for them—and you." She moved slightly, though sluggishly, to adjust her position on the bed.

"Yes," I agreed. "But then a funny thing happened. My landlord from the last house showed up and asked why I had moved out so abruptly. He was visibly upset. He also didn't look well. 'What have I done wrong?' he asked me sadly as we sipped coffee on my new front porch. 'You were such a good tenant, Michael. You made the place look good again.'"

Mariette's face wore a confused look. "But he had sold the place, hadn't he?"

"That's what I thought too, and that's exactly what I told him. 'But you sold the house, Tubby,' I said, dumbfounded by his question. His response stunned me. 'What?' he exclaimed. 'My friend, no one has bought that house from me. I was hoping *you* might!'"

I then related to Mariette the strange set of circumstances that set this in play. "It started when Tubby had become ill. I stopped visiting him once a month at his garage to hand in my rent. We used to sit and chat for a while. But when he became ill, since I didn't want to bother him, I instead handed my envelope to his secretary. When I heard the house had been sold, I decided simply to be on my way. I saw no particular reason to contact him about it. On the day I moved out, I handed my keys to his daughter, who was now working at his garage. She said nothing. Had he not been sick, he would certainly have told me the house hadn't been purchased."

Mariette smiled.

"When he pleaded with me to consider moving

back, I said to him, 'Look at this place, Tubby. It's so beautiful here. I'm sorry how it turned out, but I just did what I thought I had to do.'"

"He understood?" Mariette asked matter-of-factly.

"He did—sadly, though. He then finished his coffee and stood up. 'Well,' he said grumpily as he left, 'I know who those people are who did this, and if they now come to me to rent the house, I'm charging them *double* what I charged you.' He was really upset about it. Tubby died a week later and the house passed into the hands of his children."

"Wow," Mariette said, opening her eyes for a moment. "Those people actually helped you, even though they were obviously trying to trick you."

"They did," I agreed. "Funny how both things can be happening in the same moment," I noted.

"Now *that's* something to think about," Mariette said. "But do carry on."

"That's about it, really. Within two weeks of moving into our new home, there wasn't a mouse left to be seen on that shed roof. There were also four cats I seldom saw for a while, who also ate a lot less of their regular cat food."

Mariette smiled happily. "You all made it to cat heaven," she said softly. "It feels like this cat story has an ending now."

"Well, not quite," I said. "There was still the saga of Mr. Jack to get through before there was complete peace."

"Mr. Jack?" Her eyes opened.

"Yes, dear Mr. Jack, a rugged, sometimes mean old stray who brought many feral kittens into the world."

"I'm listening," Mariette said, inviting me to continue as she closed her eyes again. Then, speaking as if to herself, she added, "Mr. Jack sounds a bit like my father."

Mr. Jack

"I realize today that I've evolved in my relationships with cats, and I'm evolving still," I told Mariette. "I think Mr. Jack came to me so I could see this. He came to teach me how to do the right thing, even if it means doing the hard thing—and that when we do the right thing, it all turns out well for everyone."

I stood for a moment, needing to stretch my legs, then settled back down into my chair. "Mr. Jack was the neighborhood feral tomcat," I said. "He had obviously been running the show in that area long before we moved in, probably for years. He was an old grey-and-white short-haired cat with weepy eyes and a really bad attitude." I chuckled as I added, "He always had a cross expression on his face, even when he was sleeping."

I related to Mariette how Mr. Jack started stealing cat food from the kitchen. "Because he always sprayed before he left, or before I chased him out, I started putting food outside the back door to keep him from entering the house. For a while we had a truce, except for every now and then when I had to chase him off with the broom for spraying indoors. He always came back for meals, either ignoring me or giving me a dirty look. I didn't dare forget to put food out for him, or he would punish me with cat spray all over the kitchen."

"He sounds like a real terror," Mariette whispered.

"He was an annoyance, for sure—and at times a bit of a bully, on occasion giving my clan a hard time. But I wouldn't really describe him as a *terror*," I clarified. "He was just a grumpy old buck."

"What happened to him?"

"One day Mr. Jack brought his girlfriend with him—and the next thing, she brought her four kittens with her. There were now ten cats on the property! I spoke to Lynn, Aberdeen's animal angel, and she handed me a cat trap box. 'Catch them all and take them to the SPCA,' she advised. 'It's the best thing to do for everybody.' I dutifully caught the kittens, quite easily, though the mother eluded me. However, as soon as the kittens were gone, so was she, so the problem appeared resolved. For a while Mr. Jack and I continued to live in an uneasy truce sprinkled with skirmishes and rude words. Then one day Mr. Jack showed up with *two* pregnant girlfriends. Next thing, they all disappeared together."

"Sounds *just* like my father," Mariette said, opening her eyes and grinning.

I looked at her, pondering what she had said.

"No really," she chuckled, "Mr. Jack sounds just

like him." Closing her eyes again, she waved for me to go on.

"Shortly thereafter, both those females showed up again, this time each with a litter of kittens bouncing along behind them in the grass. I borrowed the cat trap once more and drove them in batches to the SPCA in Graff-Reinett, which as you know is 52 kilometers away. To catch both mothers and all their kittens took four trips. When I walked into the SPCA for the fourth time, the attendant burst out laughing. 'You must be cleaning all the strays out of your area,' she declared. 'I am, and this is the last of them,' I confirmed. 'Well,' she advised, serious now, 'make sure you catch the tomcat that's doing the deed, otherwise you're just wasting both your time and mine.'"

"She was talking about Mr. Jack."

"She was indeed. However, when the attendant inquired whether I knew who the tomcat was, I flat lied, telling her, 'Uh, I think I might have seen him around.' It was while standing there at the SPCA, lying to the woman, that I knew what I had to do. 'I'll try catching that male,' I said as I left."

"Why hadn't you had him neutered?" Mariette asked. "Wouldn't that have been the simplest solution?"

"I hadn't had Mr. Jack neutered because he was never going to be a house cat. I let him stay on the property because Lynn, the cat lover I'd known, explained to me that if you only have spayed and neutered cats, the male strays constantly fight over the territory. So I allowed Mr. Jack to hang out, thinking this would avoid that problem. But it had come with a price—and a smell! My cats never got to enjoy the front porch because Mr. Jack had made it his turf. There were also constant cat spray wars between him and Chubbis Choppis."

"Oh dear," Mariette chuckled.

"Chubbis Choppis purposely followed him around the garden, covering Mr. Jack's spray with his own scent. He had already received a few harsh thumpings from Mr. Jack. But like Monster, Chubbis Choppis was always up for a skirmish, so this didn't deter him. And, of course, there was the fact Mr. Jack was breeding like a rabbit. Anyway, early the next morning, I opened a can of sardines and waited for Mr. Jack to show up. I didn't use the cat trap box as I figured that, using the sardines, I could get him to walk right into my cat carrier."

"And did he?"

"He most certainly did, though he gave me an extremely suspicious look as he did so. I snapped the door shut and placed him in the back of my van, then drove straight to the SPCA. I knew what his fate was to be, so it wasn't an easy thing for me to do. It wasn't like he was some unknown stray. Even though he was for the most part a pain in the neck, I had known him for over a year, and the truth is I had grown to like him. On the other hand, I wasn't doing this for myself alone."

"You were doing it for the cats you had chosen to live with."

"I was. Ever since moving into our beautiful space, they'd had to live in Mr. Jack's grumpy shadow. Still, I didn't like dispatching him like this. In fact, it was the sort of thing I used to avoid doing in the past—the hard, correct thing. I only did this sort of unpleasant task when my hand was forced, like when Chubbis Choppis got so badly beaten up, or when I feared people might start confusing me with Jeff the Cat Chief."

Mariette giggled.

"As I walked toward the SPCA office, the attendant came out and put her hands on her hips. 'You got him,' she said cheerfully. 'I did,' I replied. She inspected him through the meshed door. 'He's a strong one,' she said admiringly, 'and he must be quite old too. He's had a good life, I'm sure.' Those words were obviously intended to comfort me. She then stood up and shouted to a nearby staff member, 'Colleen! Come take this cat to a kennel and put water in there too, please!' The staff member came over and picked up the carrier with quite a jolt, as if she assumed it would be much heavier. Turning, she hastily walked toward the kennels, swinging the carrier in an ungainly manner. 'That woman knows nothing about animals,' I thought. Just as I was thinking this, the wire mesh door to the carrier tumbled to the ground, with Mr. Jack following right behind. He had broken out! A lot of shouting ensued, and several staff members gave chase."

Weak as she was, Mariette raised herself onto one elbow and whispered excitedly, "Did he get away?"

"Of course, it was Mr. Jack," I chuckled, remembering him. "The SPCA woman just burst out laughing. 'You'll never catch him!' she shouted after the desperately dashing staff. Then, turning to me, she explained, 'I have never yet seen a human catch an adult cat that doesn't want to be caught.' We watched together as Mr. Jack made it effortlessly over the perimeter fencing and into the wild area that stretched down to the river. 'Well,' she chuckled, 'that cat just made it into cat heaven, which is what we call that place down there. They have loads of mice, sex, and there is the river and the trees. They are never hungry enough to come near our cat traps.'"

Mariette was giggling as she lowered herself back down, closing her eyes again and no doubt imagining the scene. As she lay quietly listening, I explained how, by the time I had arrived at the SPCA, I was surprised how clear and peaceful I had become about the task at hand.

"Of course, when Mr. Jack escaped," I continued, "the woman was most apologetic. 'Sorry about that,' she said more than once. 'Sorry you drove all this way,' she said yet again. But I wasn't sorry. I was quietly relieved. Mr. Jack wouldn't be dying that day. 'No problem. I like the way it turned out,' I said to her as I left to drive back to my own cat heaven, where all my cats were given a fresh start in their own home."

"I like the way it turned out too," Mariette whispered. "I like that Mr. Jack made it to heaven too, even though he was a bit of a scoundrel." Opening her eyes, she smiled peacefully. "Will you do me a big favor?" she asked.

"Of course," I said.

"Will you bring me some photographs of your cats as they are now? That would be a perfect Christmas present."

"I don't have any photographs," I explained. "All the pictures I have are on my laptop. But I can bring it in and show them to you that way."

"Thank you, Michael. I'd love that. Before we end today, tell me about your cats as they are today. Are they happy?"

"They have as good a life as I could possibly give them. They now hang out by the back door in the morning sun, and the smell of cat spray is a distant memory. Each has their own area of the garden, and they still catch mice every day. Mrs. Botjie is always by my side whenever she isn't curled up napping somewhere. Everything in the world belongs to her, and there's no compromising on this. She still likes to sit on the edge of the bathtub when I'm soaking."

"And Presence?"

"Presence has mostly grown out of her skittishness. She doesn't even run from the room when I switch on the vacuum cleaner. She's my storm detector though, because she still hides from thunder half an hour before

I can hear it. She has the uncanny knack of knowing when I take a siesta too, always arriving to curl up by my stomach a few minutes after I lie down."

"And Big Guy and Chubby Choppis?"

"Big Guy is the sweetest gentleman you will ever meet and has really bonded with me. If I get up at night to go to the bathroom, he has to accompany me. Then I am required to accompany him to the kitchen so he can have a snack. If he's around, he's usually the first one at my feet every morning, and his eagerness to greet me each new day always melts my heart. He also takes his mouse hunting *very* seriously. So unless it's freezing or raining outside, he's often up at first light for a healthy mouse breakfast. He reminds me so much of Mr. Pickle."

I fell silent for a moment, remembering.

"Chubbis Choppis still remains quite small and compact, and still unbearably cute. He, however, like Monster, thinks he's enormous. Although he's been severely beaten up a number of times, it doesn't deter him from taking on any cat that walks past our front gate. Chubbis Choppis also knows when it's Friday, because only on Fridays does he come in and wait in the kitchen for wet food, which I mostly only dish out on a Friday. He's still treated pretty much as an outsider by the others, but he doesn't take it personally. He's indeed the happiest cat that ever lived. I remember Mama Sita and Baba often because of his delicious presence. Every day, late afternoon, he likes to charge around the garden ecstatically, for no apparent reason at all, just out of sheer happiness."

"It sounds like they are all doing very well," Mariette whispered, looking delighted.

"They are all my heart fish, because they swim around in my heart," I said, smiling. "Also, I've purchased the property now, so hopefully none of us will have to move again."

Mariette reached out her hand. I stood up and took it. "I'd so like to see those pictures of Presence, Big Guy, Chubbis Choppis, and Mrs. Botjie. I feel I know them now. I feel I have had a whole life with your many cats. Thank you for the stories, Michael, I can really say I truly feel like *a cat person* now."

"I'll be back with the pictures," I promised, "and who knows, I might think of a cat story we missed along the way."

"The Sphinx story," she whispered. "You haven't told that one yet."

"And that's a good one," I chuckled.

She looked deep into my eyes for a moment. "You and your cats are indeed my Christmas miracle," she said, peacefully smiling. As she squeezed my hand gently, I knew she was my very special Christmas miracle too.

Epilogue

Mariette van Wyk passed away peacefully that evening. Christmas came and went without her. A year has now passed since I sat and chatted with her delightful presence in the Aberdeen Hospital. I think of her fondly each time I drive past that building on my way to a breakfast at The Padstal, and the memory of our short but deeply meaningful encounter often brings warmth to my heart when life feels cold.

I cannot think of a more uniquely beautiful place to be living than here in The Karoo, and I cannot think of a more uniquely magnificent people to surround myself with than those I today call my neighbors. I see now that the Christmas miracle I received through Cathy's invitation wasn't really about Christmas at all. What I received from spending time with Mariette, aside from the great pleasure of her charming company, was the realization that *I* have finally come home.

Every now and then, I take out the short note Mariette wrote for me and left with Nurse Thandokazi, who passed it on to me with a quiet, wordless smile and a long hug following the memorial service. When I first received the note, I waited until I was home and on my porch with a cup of coffee before reading Mariette's final words to me: "We shall meet again," she assured me, "and then you can tell me that Sphinx story! Oh, and I still might come visit you through one of your cats."

Today, I feel even closer to my cats because of Mariette's shared love for them, even though she never got to meet them. Strangely enough, Mrs. Botjie picked up a new habit shortly after Mariette's passing. At bath time, just after I climb into the tub, she insists on standing up against the side of the tub, giving me a kiss right on my lips. Then, hopping up onto the rim and leaning in, she takes a few sips of the hot bathwater. I say each time she does it, "Mrs. Botjie, is that like a nice hot cup of tea for you?"

Bye-bye Mrs. Botjie

Dearest Mrs. Botjie,

Who could have known that before this book even reached its editing phase, you would be gone. The most terrible thing that could happen, happened. In one tragic moment, one world ended and another began—a world without beautiful you in it.

It's six months since that day, the last day of the year, when you dashed under the back tire of the car as I reversed out the gate. I still tear up when I feel your presence and absence. Reversing out the gate still occasionally ambushes me with body-jolting memories of that awful moment. However, through the horror of it all, there was so much obvious grace.

You see, Mrs. Botjie, I sensed you were leaving. You knew you were leaving too. For about three weeks before that terrible day, I noticed how you suddenly quieted, to the point I would come looking for you, when it was normally the other way round. You gently began dissolving our shared routines.

I noted how you spent more and more time sleeping

on your red swivel office chair on the back porch where the afternoon sun wipes the walls with delicious warmth. I so loved coming out there to visit you, peeking playfully around the corner, knowing you would awaken, look up, and say your name for me, "Mu." I seldom ever heard you meow. It just wasn't your way to be ordinary. You had different words for different moments, and you kept all visitors entertained with your intent to be the center of attention and conversation.

I am so glad I consciously soaked in each moment with you in those last few weeks when I sensed a big change coming. I am so glad I got to tell you over and over how much I appreciate and love you. Standing quietly with you in my arms on the porch watching the sheets of rain from a passing thunderstorm is a perfect moment tattooed forever into my heart.

As I write these words, I realize this is the first time I am writing without you here to oversee each sentence. Who would have thought such a thing could happen, Mrs. Botjie?

A strange event occurred three days after I put your body in the ground beneath the pecan tree where you loved to sit and contemplate the movement in the garden. I know it had everything to do with you. I had been playing with Big Guy early in the morning near your gravesite, when I thought I heard the phone. When I returned moments later from the false alarm, I noticed Big Guy's tail sticking out of a nearby lavender bush. I thought he was still playing hide and seek with me. But as I approached, I noted the markings on the tail were too defined, and the fur was too thick.

I fetched a bamboo pole and prodded gently, but nothing moved. Once the scented foliage was parted, Big Guy and I discovered the still-lukewarm body of a large, old, male civet cat, curled up neatly and spirit departed. The form was so beautiful to behold, so at peace. In that moment, as I gently picked up its limp body, literally three meters from where your body had been buried, I knew the question I was being asked, and so too the immense flow of grace that was being showered on me: "So Michael, which death are you to blame for?"

Shortly after this, I received a call from my mother wanting to share an experience she'd had a few days before. She said she had been startled awake in the early hours of the morning by her dog Minky leaping off her bed. After realizing nothing was amiss and that Minky had quietly curled up in her basket, she lay back down. But moments later, she felt as if something was on the end of her bed. She opened her eyes, and to her utter disbelief saw a cat sitting there, quietly staring at her. She said she bolted out of bed and immediately went in search of the intruder before Minky could get hold of it. But she found no cat. Then, as she made herself a cup of tea, it dawned on her that it was you, Mrs. Botjie, coming to say goodbye. She thought I was too upset to tell me about it at the time. She was right. My mother says she doesn't really feel comfortable around cats, but that she adored you, Mrs. Botjie. Everybody who met you did. You insisted.

You let me see you twice too, as clear as day, on the windowsill in the lounge and in the garden near the pecan tree. I knew both times not to look directly at you. I also knew, after seeing you the second time on the windowsill in the morning sunlight, that I would not see you like that again. I was so grateful to have these two experiences.

It took months for me to remove your red swivel chair from the porch. It still had your fur all over it, and I could sit there when my eyes became rivers. I had to walk out there many times after you left to show myself that you were indeed gone. But being the way you are, you made sure to leave your mark long after that chair will be used by anyone.

I remember being so pleased when you strolled through the spilt paint and left your tan-colored paw prints sprinkled neatly across the chocolate brown tiles in the bathroom. I knew it was an important moment right as you did that. I have since clear-varnished them. I remember too the moment you strolled across the wet cement when I was resurfacing the paving. I recall clearly in that moment also being so pleased you did. I now see your signature every day. You always knew exactly what you were doing. You insisted on being seen in this world. I indeed saw you.

Time is wicked, Mrs. Botjie. It often acts like

sandpaper upon our fragile memories, wearing them into worn reflections and tattered forgetfulness. But time will not win here. I shall not forget you. I will remember you were in this world long after I forget most of the people I have met. I will always remember how we walked together in the pouring rain when all the other cats cowered from the thunder. I so appreciated that you came every evening when I got into bed to say goodnight, and how you were there the second I stirred in the morning to accompany me into each new day. Every day you chose me, no matter what state I was in. Right from the start of our story together, you chose me.

When the mind cannot accept, the heart has to move forward for a while until everything can catch up. It was the 3rd or 4th of January before I registered a whole New Year had begun. I was as altered by your sudden departure as my entire life has been by your ten-year presence in it. Thank you for loving me more deeply than I could ever have deserved. I know you will be back in some form or another—and I know that when that reunion comes knocking, I will recognize you as clearly as you did me back with Ingrid in the cat pound.

Big Guy, Presence, and Chubbis Choppis do well to cover for you, but you are not replaced. There is and will only ever be one Mrs. Botjie. In some strange, inexplicable way, I know this book is a parting gift from you to me. You even have the absolute final word written in it. Thank you for being my heart fish. We had a good life together, my friend—the very best.

I know you loved your time in the garden, and I am glad I see your resting place every day as I go about my activities here without you to oversee each and every one of them. But as has happened before, our souls shall meet again. And with all things being as they are, for the time being, it's likely that Mariette has a truly attentive cat with her in heaven.

Bye-bye, beautiful Mrs. Botjie.

Your very best friend,

Mu